The Dwarves of Death

JONATHAN COE

PENGUIN BOOKS

PENGUIN BOOKS

Published by the Penguin Group
Penguin Books Ltd, 27 Wrights Lane, London w8 5tz, England
Penguin Putnam Inc., 375 Hudson Street, New York, New York 10014, USA
Penguin Books Australia Ltd, Ringwood, Victoria, Australia
Penguin Books Canada Ltd, 10 Alcorn Avenue, Toronto, Ontario, Canada m4v 3b2
Penguin Books India (P) Ltd, 11 Community Centre,
Panchsheel Park, New Delhi – 110 017, India
Penguin Books (NZ) Ltd, Cnr Rosedale and Airborne Roads,
Albany, Auckland, New Zealand
Penguin Books (South Africa) (Pty) Ltd, 5 Watkins Street,
Denver Ext 4, Johannesburg 2094, South Africa

Penguin Books Ltd, Registered Offices: Harmondsworth, Middlesex, England

First published by Fourth Estate Ltd 1990
Published in Penguin Books 2001

1

Set in 11/13 Monotype Dante
Typeset by Intype London Ltd
Printed in England by Clays Ltd, St Ives plc

PENGUIN BOOKS

The Dwarves of Death

Jonathan Coe was born in Birmingham in 1961. He has published five novels, *The Accidental Woman*, *A Touch of Love*, *The Dwarves of Death*, *What a Carve Up!*, which won the 1995 John Llewellyn Rhys Prize, and *The House of Sleep*, which won the 1998 Prix Médicis Étranger. They are all available in Penguin. His latest novel, *The Rotters' Club*, is published in Viking. He is currently writing a biography of the novelist B. S. Johnson.

Thanks are due to the following people: Ralph Pite, for writing the words to 'Madeline/Stranger In A Foreign Land'; Brian Priestley, for copying out 'Tower Hill' and teaching me most of what little I know about music; Michael Blackburn, for publishing 'Middle Eight' in the first issue of his *Sunk Island Review*; Janine McKeown, Paul Daintry, Andrew Hodgkiss and Tony Peake for inspiration and help; and Kinmor Music (publishers) and Tom Ross (translator) for permission to quote from 'Fadachd an t-seòladair' ('The Sailor's Longing') by John McLennan: the version William hears as he stands outside Karla's window being from Christine Primrose's wonderful LP *'S tu nam chuimhne*, available on Temple Records (TP024).

The epigraphs in this book are reproduced by kind permission of Warner Chappell Music Ltd. Words and music: Morrissey and Johnny Marr © Morrissey and Marr Songs Ltd.

Contents

Nuair chi mi eun a' falbh air sgiath,
Bu mhiann leam bhith 'na chuideachd:
Gu'n deanainn cùrs' air tìr mo rùin,
Far bheil an sluagh ri fuireach.

Intro

this night has opened my eyes
and I will never sleep again

MORRISSEY,
This Night Has Opened My Eyes

I find it hard to describe what happened.

It was late in the afternoon, on a far from typical London Saturday. Winter was mild that year, I remember, and although by 4.30 it was already good and dark, it wasn't cold. Besides, Chester had the heater on. It was broken, and you either had it on full blast or not at all. The rush of hot air was making me sleepy. I don't know if you know that feeling, when you're in a car – and it doesn't have to be a particularly comfortable car or any-thing – but you're drowsy, and perhaps you're not looking forward to the moment of arrival, and you feel oddly settled and happy. You feel as though you could sit there in that passenger seat for ever. It's a form of living for the present, I suppose. I wasn't very good at living for the present in those days: cars and trains were about the only places I could do it.

So I was sitting there, with my eyes half closed, listening to Chester crunching the gears and giving it too much throttle. I was pleased with myself that day, I must admit. I thought I'd made some good decisions. Small ones, like getting up early, having a bath, having a proper breakfast, getting the laundry done, and then getting up to Samson's to hear their lunchtime pianist. And then the bigger ones, as I sat alone at a table, drinking orange juice and letting 'Stella By Starlight' wash over me. I decided not to phone Madeline after all, to let her contact me for once. I'd sent her the tape, and made my intentions pretty clear, so now it was up to her to make some sort of response. I'd got one unit left on my phonecard, and I could use it to phone Chester instead. That was the other thing: I'd decided to take him up on his offer. I didn't owe the other members of the band anything. I needed a change of scene, a new environment. Musically, I mean. We'd grown stale and tired and it was time to get out. So I left just before the final number, round about three, and phoned Chester from a box on Cambridge Circus, and asked him what time he wanted me to come over.

'Come now,' he said. 'Come to the flat and then I can give you a lift. They're rehearsing at six so you can come and meet them all first. They all want to meet you.'

'They're rehearsing tonight? What – you want me to sit in?'

'See how it goes. See how you feel.'

Before taking the tube up to Chester's I stood at Cambridge Circus for a while and watched the people. I watched while the sky turned from blue to black and I don't think I've ever felt so good about London, before or since. I felt I'd reached some kind of turning point. Everyone else was still rushing around, panic on their faces, and I'd managed to stop, somehow, to find some time to think and take a new direction. That's how it felt, anyway, for about half an hour. I would never have believed that things were going to get even worse.

'You're not nervous about meeting these boys, are you?' Chester asked me, as we drove on into ever darker side streets.

'What are they like?'

He gave one of his short laughs, and said, in that funny, friendly North London drawl: 'Like I said, they're a bit weird.'

'Who's the one I saw that time?'

Chester gave me a sidelong glance, and I wondered whether I'd been tactless to mention it. But then he answered, readily enough: 'That was Paisley. He sings, and writes the words. He's good, too. You know, he's got real presence. He looks really manic on stage, throwing himself about. I just wish I could keep him off the drugs. It's the same with all of them. It's costing me a fortune. Perhaps you'll be a good influence on them. Someone sort of straight like you, you know – perhaps it'll set them an example. Like, Paisley, he hasn't written a song for two months. He's been too stoned.'

The car lurched and made a sickening grinding noise as Chester negotiated the difficult business of arriving at a main road, stopping, starting and crossing it.

'You ought to get this thing seen to,' I said.

'Well, I've been meaning to. Like, when the money starts coming in, right, from this band and everything. I'm going to have it done up. Or maybe get a new one. I'm just a bit hard up right now.'

Chester drove a 1973 Marina, orange. The sidelights didn't work and the heating was broken and there was something wrong with third gear, and yet somehow (like its owner) it inspired trust in spite of appearances. You knew that one day it was going to let you down, badly let you down, but perversely you continued to rely on it. It amazed me to think that the car was only a few years younger than Chester himself. He was only twenty-one; but for some reason I've always looked up to people younger than me.

'Nearly there,' he said.

We were driving down a handsome, sad sort of road, with high Georgian terraces on either side. It was that hour of the evening when the lights are on but the curtains are not yet drawn, and through the windows I could see families and couples, bathed in a golden glow, preparing their suppers, pouring their drinks. You could almost smell the basil and the bolognese sauce. We were in North

4

Islington. I felt a sudden desire to be inside one of those houses, to be either cooking or being cooked for, and all at once I realized that I had not made a proper decision today at all. I began to wish that I had phoned Madeline, and I knew that I would, at the first opportunity. I ached for her after just one week's absence. And that was the first sign that things weren't quite as simple as I'd thought.

The next sign was when Chester parked the car, pointed up at a window, and said, 'Good. They're in.'

I looked up and saw, not a soft square of amber, framing a domestic scene, but a curious, distant, flickering beam of pure white. It was luminous but muted, eerie. I must have stared at it long enough for Chester to get out and open the door on my side.

'I'm warning you, it's a bit of a tip, this place,' he said. 'The landlord doesn't care what they do to this house. He doesn't give a toss.' He found his keys and locked the door. 'When I was looking for a house for them, I heard about this place through a friend. Well, perhaps friend isn't the word. Through a business associate, if you like.' He chuckled, for some reason. 'Anyway, the deal was, he didn't mind what kind of a mess they made of it, so long as he was able to use it himself now and again. Just sort of one evening a week. Well, I knew that was ideal for these boys, 'cause I knew, any place they moved into, they'd have it looking like a pigsty in no time. So, I mean, it sounded like a dodgy deal to me, but handy with it.'

'What does he want to use it for himself?'

5

Chester shrugged. 'Search me.'

'Doesn't anyone ever see him?'

'Nope.' He looked up at the window again. 'Listen to that bloody racket. I don't know how the neighbours put up with it.'

Incredibly loud music was issuing from behind the barely lit window. A wail and swirl of saxes and synths and this drum machine pounding out some robotic backbeat. The noise in the adjoining houses must have been unbearable.

Chester went up to the front door, which was falling off its hinges, and began pounding on it with both fists.

'You have to do this,' he said, 'or they won't hear you.'

While we were waiting for someone to answer, I mentioned a matter which had been worrying me.

'Look, Chester, if I decide to join this band, then The Alaska Factory – you know, they'll fold up. I won't have time to play with them, too, and I don't think they could carry on without me.'

'Yes, I know. That's all right.'

'But we're your only two acts. It'll halve your income.'

'I've got other money coming in. Besides, what am I making out of you at the moment? Two gigs a week, at ten per cent of fifty quid a time? I've told you before, there's no money in live music, it's all in the record deal and you boys are never going to get a record deal. Are you? I mean, when did you ever make a decent demo?'

I fingered the tape in my pocket – the one we had

made only last week, the one we had made for Madeline. But all I said was: 'So?'

'Whereas this lot, you know, they've got potential. They've got image. They're *young*.' He went back down the steps into the street, and looked up at the window. 'This is bloody ridiculous. Oy!'

Cupping his hands and shouting did no good either. Finally a handful of pebbles thrown hard at the window brought a puzzled pale face, with long red hair dangling over the sill. He smiled when he saw Chester.

'Hi!'

'Are you going to let us in, or aren't you?'

'I'm sorry, Chess. We can't hear much, with the music.'

'Well hurry up, will you? It's freezing out here.'

In fact I think I was the colder of the two, in my thin old raincoat, whereas Chester, as usual, looked impeccable: fur-lined gloves, leather jacket, cloth cap, with those steely round eyes and stocky figure which seemed ready to take on anyone. He tutted to me and rubbed his hands together briskly. Then the door was yanked open, at last, by someone I recognized: it was Paisley – taller, more angular, more sallow even than I had remembered him.

'Hi, Chess,' he said. 'Come in.'

'About time too,' said Chester, as we stepped inside. 'Paisley, this is Bill.'

'Hi.' He shook my hand coldly.

'We've already met,' I said. Chester coughed, and Paisley looked puzzled, so I added: 'Briefly, down at the Goat. Remember?'

'No,' said Paisley. 'Sorry.'

We picked our way down a dark corridor, past a rusty bed frame standing against a wall, and several black bin liners from which rubbish was overflowing on to the floor.

'Watch out for the holes,' said Paisley, as he led us up the staircase. Two of the stairs were missing.

Chester turned to me and whispered: 'Is it all right to introduce you as Bill?'

'I prefer William,' I said. 'It's . . . well, it's not so short.'

'OK.'

I paused at the first landing. A window pane had been smashed and broken glass was still scattered over the floorboards. Already the music from upstairs was getting oppressively loud and a curious filthy smell had begun to infect the air, so I put my head out of the empty window frame for a little while, looking at the tidy back gardens of the other houses. Chester went on ahead, while Paisley waited for me further up the stairs.

'You coming up?'

On the second floor, the mystery of the luminous glow was solved. Paisley led me into a large room – two rooms knocked together, in fact, running the length of the house. There were no carpets, no curtains, no furniture at all except for a huge dining-table and six or seven wooden chairs. On the mantelpiece in the back half of the room was the only source of light: a long phosphorescent tube, obviously pinched from the strip lighting of some office or tube station or something. It gave off a ghostly sheen, scarcely touching the shadows in the corners of the room but throwing into unearthly relief the faces of the four people sitting around the table: three men and a woman. They were eating a massive takeaway meal: tin cartons, paper buckets and bits of old newspaper littered the table and the immediate floor area, which led me to believe that the meal was a compound of Chinese, Kentucky Fried and fish and chips. The air was thick with the smell of stale dope. There was an electric cooker in one corner; all four rings were on, which seemed to be a way of providing heat as well as making it easy to light up. My arrival had no impact. They went on drinking and smoking as if I wasn't there.

In the front half of the room, nearest the street, was the stereo system. Not a domestic hi-fi, but a huge disco console with twin turntables, mixing desk and 200-watt speakers. The noise of that maniacal, volcanic music was deafening. I put my fingers to my ears and Chester, noticing this, tactfully turned it down a little before announcing to the room in general: 'OK everyone, this is William. William's going to be your new keyboard player, right. William – meet The Unfortunates.'

There was a muted grunt from one or two of the eaters. The woman looked my way. That was it.

'Hi,' I said nervously. 'Nice place you've got here.'

This produced a short outburst of mirthless laughter.

'Yeah, it's got character, hasn't it?' somebody said.

'Sometimes you can smell the character of this place half-way down the street.'

I decided to try another subject.

'Is this one of your tapes?' I asked.

'What, this music? No. It's too tuneful for us, this is. We used to sound like this, when we were trying to be commercial.'

Chester switched it off.

'Here, I'll put one of their tapes on,' he said.

What I heard was disconcerting, but if you listened closely, there was a kind of sense behind it. The rhythm section was loud, fast and minimal, while the two guitar-ists – one using some sort of fuzz box, the other playing strange funk patterns high up the neck – seemed to be playing songs all of their own. Meanwhile, Paisley's voice was jack-knifing all over the place, from the top to the bottom of the register:

> Death is life
> Death is life
> And black is the colour of the human heart
> Death is life
> Death is life
> You have to die before you can live
> You have to kill before you can love

'Nice lyrics,' I said to Paisley, when it came to an end. 'Did you write them?'

'Yeah. You think so? I don't like them. Too soppy.'

'Yeah, you want to . . . darken them up a bit,' said

someone at the table. 'We don't want to start sounding too friendly.'

'We don't sound too friendly, do we?' Paisley asked me.

'It's not your main problem.'

'You think you could do something with that?' Chester asked. 'Put some keyboards in, I mean?'

'Yes, sure.'

'Something with a bit of bite, I mean. No strings or anything. We don't want it to sound like Mantovani, you know what I mean?'

'I think so. Listen, Chester – ' I felt in my pocket, and my fingers closed on the tape. 'I've brought something of my own along: that tape we made, last week? I know you haven't heard it yet, but – well, I think it's really good. Can I put it on? Give everyone an idea of the kind of thing I do.'

Chester shook his head.

'Not now, eh? They might think you were being pushy. Maybe play it when we go down to the studio.' He looked at his watch. 'Which had better be now. All right, everybody! Clear that shit away and get the gear downstairs. We're going to start on time for once.'

To my surprise, there was a slow but positive response. They got to their feet (leaving the remains of the meal as it was) and began putting on coats and picking up instrument cases. I've never been able to understand authority. Some people (like Chester) have it, and others (like me) don't. It's not even as if he was especially tall. As they got ready, he stood there counting heads and making a mental calculation.

'Janice, are you coming with us tonight?'

'I thought I would, yes.'

'We'll need two cars. Paisley, have you got yours outside?'

'Mm-hm.'

'Give William a lift, will you?'

'Sure.'

Soon they were all heading downstairs, leaving just Paisley and me.

'What are you waiting for?' Chester asked him.

'Finish my joint.'

'For God's sake, Paisley. It costs me five quid an hour, that place. Every time, we lose an hour for some reason or other. Usually to do with you.' He turned to me. 'Don't let him be late, Bill. See you in a few minutes.'

His footsteps echoed down the staircase. From the street, there was the sound of car doors opening and closing. Then the car drove away.

Paisley got slowly to his feet, bent down to a wall socket and turned off the light. He turned all the rings on the cooker off, too, and then sat down.

'What are you doing?' I asked.

It was completely dark. All I could see was the yellow glint of his eyeballs, the shine of the grease on his jet-black hair, and the tip of his joint glowing as he inhaled.

'Want some?' he said, leaning forward.

I walked to the window.

'You heard what Chester said. We'd better go. Are you safe to drive after taking that stuff?'

'We're not going yet. Got some business to do first.'

'Business?'

'C'mere.'

I guessed that he was beckoning, so I went to the table and sat opposite him.

'Chester tell you about our landlord?'

'A bit.'

'He's a dealer. Uses this place to meet people. That's why we rehearse on Saturdays, see – he wants us to be out of the house.'

'And?'

'There was a phone call for him this morning. First thing. Nobody else was up. Then I got this idea, see.'

Not wanting to know, I asked: 'What idea?'

'I pretended to be him, didn't I? 'Cause they said, "Is that Mr Jones?" – I mean, a name like that, it's a cover, isn't it? No one's really got a name like that – and I said, "Yes, speaking." So they said, "Meet you at the house tonight, six-thirty," and I said, "What for?", and they said, "We got some stuff for you," and I said, "What sort of stuff?", and they said, "Good stuff," and I said, "How much stuff?", and they said, "Loads of stuff, mate, loads," and I said, "All right, I'll be here," and they said, "Make sure none of them wankers is in," and I said, "It's all right, I'll be here on my own," and then they rang off.'

'I don't get it,' I said.

13

'Well, I've got this plan, see.'

Still not wanting to know, I said: 'What plan?'

'Well look. They're going to turn up with all this stuff, right, and they're going to want some money for it. The thing is, I'm going to take the stuff, not give them any money, and then scarper.' There was a pause. 'What do you think?'

'That's your plan?'

'Yeah.'

'Look, Paisley, how many of those things have you had today?'

We waited in silence for several minutes. Every time a car approached my heart began to beat frantically. It was an absurd situation. Why could my life never be simple? All I had wanted to do was audition with a new band. Why should it have to involve something like this?

'Paisley, this is a stupid idea,' I said at last. 'Let's go and join the others. I mean, if you really think these guys are going to come in here and calmly hand over – look, how old are you?'

'Eighteen.'

'Jesus, you're only eighteen, you don't want to be mixed up in all this. You don't want to be into drugs and crime at your age. You want to be a *singer*, for God's sake. You've got a terrific voice, you've got a manager who's devoted to you – '

'You think I've got a good voice?'

'Of course you have. Look, you don't need me to tell you that.'

He frowned. 'I don't know. Sometimes it doesn't sound so good.'

'Listen, we've got a singer in our band, right? To him, you're like – Sinatra. You're like Nat King Cole. Marvin Gaye. Robert Wyatt.'

'You mean that?'

'We've just made this new tape. Here, have a listen to this.' I took the cassette out of my pocket and handed it to him in the dark. 'Listen to what he sounds like. I mean, he's OK, it's not embarrassing or anything. But just think what you could do with a song like that.'

'What – is this something you wrote yourself?'

'Yes. It's . . . well, it's a very personal song, actually. I'd like you to hear it and . . . maybe hear you sing it some time.'

Just then, a car stopped outside the house. Two doors slammed.

'Here they are.'

He slipped the cassette into his jacket pocket, stood up and went to the window overlooking the street. Quietly, I joined him, and saw the car parked outside, with its sidelights still on.

'Can you see them?'

I thought I saw figures moving in the shadows by the front door; but couldn't be certain. The next thing we knew, there were footsteps in the corridor.

'Two people,' I said.

Now that I could see his face, Paisley looked scared; more scared even than I felt.

'Have you any idea what you're going to do?'

'Ssh.'

From downstairs, a voice called: 'Hello!'

Paisley went to the door and, doing his best to disguise his voice, shouted, 'Up here!'

The footsteps ascended the stairs, slowly. We heard a thud and a cry of 'Shit!' where the missing boards must have been. Paisley withdrew to the centre of the room, where the wall had been knocked out. I stayed right where I was, beside the window.

The footsteps stopped on the first landing, and we heard one voice say, 'It's a bit bloody dark in here, isn't it?'

'Shut up,' said the other.

'We're upstairs!' Paisley called. His voice was shaking now.

The footsteps approached, getting slower and slower. Outside our room, they stopped.

'In here,' said Paisley.

*

I find it hard to describe what happened. There was a long silence, a very long silence, and then some more footsteps. Suddenly, two figures were framed in the doorway. They stood apart, threatening and wordless, their little bodies visible only in silhouette. They were wearing hoods and carrying heavy wooden clubs, and they could only have been about three feet tall, both of them. I don't know how long they must have stood there. Paisley just stared at them, frozen with shock and terror, until they stepped forward and began to scream, together. This awful, icy, high-pitched scream. All at once they were running towards him, and then one of them jumped on to the table. The other one was swinging his club around and starting to hit Paisley about the legs with it. Paisley turned, and from somewhere or other he produced a knife and started slashing madly in the air. He was shouting something, too. I don't know what. Then he must have managed to knife the little man in the hand because he dropped his club and started screaming and shouting 'Fuck! Fuck! Fuck!' and he grabbed the bottom of Paisley's jacket and tried to pull him down. But by now the other one, the one on the table, was standing right over Paisley, and before I could warn him or anything, he'd crunched him over the head, and there was this sound like an egg-shell cracking when you're making an omelette. And then Paisley was on the floor, and for the next minute or so they were both at it, beating the life out of him till there was nothing left of his head at all and they were both too tired to do any more.

They still hadn't noticed that I was there. I was stooped beneath the window sill – not a very good idea, when you think about it, because it put me at eye-level with them – but it must have been too dark for them to make me out. I just crouched there and looked at these two little figures standing over Paisley's body. One of them had his wounded hand clasped between his knees: he must have been in agony.

'Come on now,' the other one said. 'Let's get out of here.'

This produced no response other than an indistinct mutter, followed by a moan.

'Come on, for Christ's sake. Let's get you down to the car.'

'The jacket.'

'What?'

'We'll have to take his jacket. It's got my blood on it, and my prints.'

'Jesus Christ.'

He dropped his club, rolled Paisley's body over and got the jacket off as best he could.

'And his trousers. It's all over his trousers, look.'

So they took off his trousers, too, and wrapped them around the still-bleeding hand.

'Come on, let's get shot of this place. Let's go.'

Just as they were leaving, the injured one paused, reflectively. He shook his head and said: 'I didn't enjoy that much.'

'Me neither.'

And then they clattered off down the stairs, these two little men, leaving me to shake and shiver beneath the window, alone with Paisley's corpse. I heard their two car doors opening, and heard the car drive off even before the doors had had time to close.

I stayed there for a while, God knows how long. I didn't go anywhere near the body, though. I didn't even step over it – I skirted right round it, giving it as wide a berth as the room would allow. Then I too climbed down the stairs; slowly, one at a time, clutching at the banister. When I got to the front door I stood in the doorway, drinking in the fresh air. I don't think, at that point, that my mind had taken in what I'd just seen.

I guessed, afterwards, that the police must have had their eye on that house for quite some time. Perhaps they'd even been tapping the phone or something. The first thing I saw when I stepped outside, anyway, was a police car tearing down the street in my direction. Before I knew what was happening it had pulled up at the front door; so the two of them must have got a good look at my face as I stood there wondering what the hell I was supposed to do next. Then, after a few fatal moments of indecision, my brain stuttered into action again. In the time it took them to get out of the car, I realized that no explanation I could give for my presence would stop them from suspecting me of being involved in the crime; perhaps of having committed it myself.

So I turned and ran back up the stairs. I could hear them coming after me. When I reached the first landing I remembered the broken window, clambered through it and crouched, ready to jump. I'm sure they would have got me, sure they would have caught up with me, if it hadn't been for those missing stairs. There was the sound of wood giving way and a cry of pain and I knew that one of them had fallen through.

'Are you all right?' his mate was calling. 'Are you all right?'

This was my chance. I jumped and landed in the middle of all this long wet soft grass. The whole garden was like a jungle. I ran right to the bottom, scrambling and tripping over brambles, branches, old broken milk bottles – all sorts of junk – and then at the end I climbed over the wall and found myself in a quiet, unlit alleyway.

I was more terrified than I had ever been in my life. Much more. So although I was tired, it wasn't difficult to carry on running. While I was running, you see, I couldn't stop to think.

*

I wanted to get the difficult part out of the way – to describe what happened, that evening in Islington. The temptation now, of course, is to go straight on and tell you how it all ended, but there are a few things I have to explain first. I have to explain about Madeline, and Karla, and London, and why I wanted to join Paisley's band in the first place. It's hard to know where to start – hard to know if there was a specific point where things started to go downhill. But I think there was. It can be traced back to a particular evening, and to a particular culprit. Yes, I know where to point the finger of accusation.

Because it all started, as far as I'm concerned, with Andrew Lloyd Webber.

Theme One

Boy afraid
prudence never pays

and everything she wants costs money

MORRISSEY,
Girl Afraid

Why do I dislike the music of Andrew Lloyd Webber so much? I suppose for the same reason that I dislike London: because everybody else flocks to it as if it were the only thing worth experiencing on earth. Take that night at *Phantom of the Opera*. It was a Thursday evening, more than two weeks before the events which I've just described. I hadn't seen Madeline for days and I was really looking forward to being with her again. We should have been having fun; instead it was a disaster. And it was all that bastard's fault.

Oh, there were some OK moments, I suppose. A nice cadence in 'Think of Me' which sounded remarkably like

Puccini's 'O Mio Bambino Caro', and a recurring phrase which made me think insistently, for some reason, of Prokofiev's *Cinderella*. But I couldn't stand the way he jumbled it all together with no concern for style, for period, for genre – bits of pastiche operetta leading into passages of lumpen rock music, and endless chromatic scales on a Gothic-sounding organ which would still have seemed like a cliché forty years ago if you'd heard them on the soundtrack to a Universal B-movie. And yet the audience lapped it up. They couldn't get enough of it. I just cannot understand this phenomenon.

And what a hassle, what a ridiculous, exhausting palaver I'd had to go through just to listen to that load of old nonsense. Have you any idea how hard it is to get tickets to that show? Did Madeline have any idea when she suggested it, I wondered? After endless enquiries at the box office, I was told that my best bet was to come along on the day itself, early. So I joined the queue at five o'clock in the morning – *five o'clock*, do you hear me – behind a bunch of Japanese businessmen, and I stayed until nearly half past ten (which made me two hours late for work) only to see the last set of tickets go to some people five places ahead of me in the queue. So then I phoned some agency in my lunch hour, and they said they did have some tickets – returns or something – but I could only have them if I came over and paid for them in person, and then they fished these things from under the counter and I ended up shelling out ninety pounds (I feel ill just thinking about it) for two seats. So you can imagine what sort of mood I was in by the time I met Madeline at the theatre, and things didn't improve when we took our seats – which were quite good ones, actually – and just as the show was about to start, this six-foot monster came and sat right in front of me, so that for the whole evening all I had a view of was the back of his neck. I couldn't see a damn thing. I might just as well have stayed at home and listened to the record.

Not that I paid much attention to the music anyway, to be honest. A date with Madeline was always a special occasion, and most of the time I was thinking about what we would do afterwards, whether we would go for a drink, what I'd say to her, whether she would let me kiss her. I'm sure that better composers than Andrew Lloyd Webber have suffered from the fact that shows and concerts are ten per cent works of art, and ninety per cent stopping-off points in a mating ritual. It's funny to think of someone like Debussy agonizing over the orchestration of some bar or other of *Pelléas et Mélisande*, not realizing that most of the men in the audience would be too busy wondering whether they could get away with putting a hand on their girlfriend's knee to even bother listening to the music. You can't help it, it's natural. Every move she made, every little unconscious gesture was more interesting to me than anything that was happening on the stage (not that I could see any of it). That bit, for instance, which is supposed to have everybody gasping, when the chandelier suddenly comes right down from the top of the theatre – there was a time when Madeline scratched her cheek which was far more exciting than that. I was conscious of every little change in the distance between us. Every time she leaned towards me my heart beat faster. At one point she bent over, close to my side, and I thought, my God, she's actually going to touch me. But her shoe had come off, and she was just putting it on again.

Three long hours later, we were outside, out in the middle of a wet, cold and noisy London night. Taxis and buses dawdled past, their tyres splashing and hissing, their headlamps reflecting on the surface of the road.

I thought, what the hell, and slid my arm beneath Madeline's. As usual, she offered neither resistance nor encouragement. She merely let it stay there, and I didn't have the nerve to follow it up by taking her hand. We had been going out for nearly six months.

'Well . . .' I said at last, as we began strolling, for no particular reason, towards Piccadilly Circus.

'Did you enjoy that?' she asked.

'Did you?'

'Yes. I really enjoyed it. I thought it was wonderful.'

I squeezed her arm.

'You've got a good sense of humour,' I said.

'How do you mean?'

'It's one of the things I like about you. Your sense of humour. I mean, we can laugh together. You say something ironic, and I know exactly what you mean.'

'I wasn't being ironic. I really did enjoy it.'

'There you go again. Double irony: I love it. You know,

it's a great thing when two people share a sense of humour, it really . . . shows something about them.'

'William, I'm not being ironic. I enjoyed myself tonight. It was a good show. You understand?'

We had stopped walking. We had pulled apart and were facing one another.

'Are you serious? You liked it?'

'Yes, didn't you? What was wrong with it?'

We started walking again. Apart, this time.

'The music was facile and unmemorable. It was harmonically primitive and melodically derivative. The plot relied on cheap emotional effects and crude pathos. The staging was showy, manipulative and deeply reactionary.'

'You mean you didn't enjoy it?'

For a second I was looking straight into her sad grey eyes. But I still shook my head.

'No.' We walked on in silence. 'I mean, what did you like about it?'

'I don't know. Why do you always have to analyse things? It was . . . it was good.'

'Terrific. I see. Tell me, what did you do about that invitation to appear on *Critics' Forum*? Did you ever answer that?'

'I don't know what you're talking about. I haven't been invited anywhere.'

'Can't you tell when I'm being ironic?'

'No.'

We had nearly arrived at Piccadilly Circus. We stopped

outside Pizzaland. I could see that I had upset her, but couldn't find it in me to do anything about it.

'What do you want to do now?' I asked.

'I don't mind.'

'Do you want to go for a drink?'

'I don't mind.'

'Come on.' I took her arm again and began leading her towards Soho. 'You know, it would be nice if you expressed an opinion sometimes. It would make life easier. Instead of leaving all the decisions to me.'

'I just expressed an opinion, and you made fun of me. Where are we going, anyway?'

'I thought we'd go to Samson's. Is that OK?'

'Fine. You want to listen to your friend again, do you?'

'He might be there tonight, I don't know.' In fact Tony had phoned me only the day before. I knew full well he was going to be playing there that evening. 'Do you have to call him "my friend"? You know his name, don't you?'

I was so much in love with Madeline that sometimes, at work, I would begin to shiver just thinking about her: I would shake with panic and pleasure, and end up dropping piles of records and stacks of tapes all over the place. For this reason it didn't use to matter to me that we never got on particularly well. Bickering with Madeline was more desirable to me than making love to any other woman in the world. The idea of us being happy together – lying in the same bed, say, silent and half-asleep – seemed so beautiful that I couldn't even begin to visualize it. In my heart I was sure it would never happen, and meanwhile to exchange grumpy remarks with her on a cold winter's evening in the nastier end of Soho seemed privilege enough. I doubt if she felt the same way; but then how exactly *did* she feel?

She always was an enigma to me, and I'm not going to make out some perverse theory that this was part of the attraction. It used to piss me off no end. All the time I knew Madeline, there was always the sense that she didn't fit – with me, with London, with the rest of the world. I noticed it the first time I saw her: she looked so out of place, in that gloomy bar where I was playing the piano. I'd been in London for nearly a year, and I'd thought that this might turn out to be my first break. A place in some side street just off the Fulham Road that had a clapped-out baby grand and called itself a 'jazz club': I saw an advert they had placed in *The Stage* and they offered me twenty pounds cash and three non-alcoholic cocktails of my choice to play there on a Wednesday night. I turned up at six, scared out of my mind, knowing that I had to play for five hours with a repertoire of six standards and a few pieces of my own – about fifty minutes' worth of material. I needn't have worried, because there was only one customer all evening. She came in at eight and stayed till the end. It was Madeline.

I couldn't believe that a woman so well dressed and so pretty could be sitting on her own in a place like that all night. Maybe if there had been other customers they would have tried to chat her up. In fact I'm sure they would. She was always getting chatted up. That night there was only me, and even I tried to chat her up, and I'd never done anything like that in my life before. But when you've been playing your own music for nearly an hour to an audience of one, and they've been clapping at the end of every number and smiling at you and even once saying, 'I liked that one', then you feel entitled. It would have seemed rude not to. So when the time came to take another break I got my drink from the bar and went over to her table, and said: 'Do you mind if I join you?'

'No. Please do.'

'Can I buy you something?'

'No thanks, I'm all right for the moment.'

She was drinking dry white wine. I sat down on a stool opposite her, not wanting to appear too forward.

'Is it always this quiet in here?' I asked.

'I don't know. I've never been here before.'

'It's a bit tacky, isn't it? For the area, I mean.'

'It's only just opened. It'll probably take a while to get off the ground.'

She was so lovely. She had short blonde hair and a grey fitted jacket, a woollen skirt that came just above the knee and black silk stockings – nothing provocative, you understand, just tasteful. She had little gold studded ear-rings and lipstick which probably only seemed such a dark red because her complexion was so pale. I noticed right away that her mouth could go in an instant from the roundest and happiest of smiles to this more habitual, downward, melancholy look. Her voice was high and musical and her pronunciation – like everything else about her – showed that she was from some high-powered background. Her hands were small and white, and she didn't paint her fingernails.

'I like the way you play the piano,' she said. 'Are you going to play here every week?'

'I don't know. It depends.' (I never did play there again, as it turned out.) 'Are you . . . are you waiting for someone? Or are you just here on your own?'

'I often go to places on my own,' she said, but added: 'Actually I was supposed to be seeing someone tonight, we were supposed to be going out for a meal. But then he phoned up and cancelled, and I'd already got myself ready, so I didn't feel like staying in. I thought I'd come and see what this place is like.'

'That was inconsiderate of him.'

'He's an old friend. I don't mind.'

'You live near here?'

'Yes, not far. South Kensington. What about you?'

'Oh, it's like another world to me, an area like this. I live in South East London. On a council estate.'

After a pause, she said: 'Do you mind if I ask you for something? A request, I mean. A piece of music.'

I felt a sudden tight grip of anxiety. You see, the reason I never made it as a cocktail bar pianist was that my repertoire was never wide enough, and I was hopeless at playing by ear. Customers are always asking pianists to play things and the only way I could have covered myself against situations like this was by learning every standard in the book. That would have taken months. It usually took me a few hours to get a piece into shape, sometimes more. Take 'My Funny Valentine', for instance. It's not a difficult tune, yet something about the middle eight had been defeating me and it had just taken me two days to get it sounding exactly how I wanted. I'd been listening to some of the most famous records, seeing how the masters had handled it and working out what I thought were some pretty neat substitutions of my own. I could play it well, now, I thought, but that had been the result of two days' hard work, and anything she was to ask for, even if I knew roughly how the tune went, was bound to come out sounding amateurish and embarrassing.

'Well . . . try me,' I still said, for some reason.

'Do you know "My Funny Valentine"?'

I frowned. 'Well . . . the title's familiar. I'm not very quick at picking things up, though. Can you remind me how it goes?'

Wouldn't anybody have done the same thing?

I think that was the best version I've ever played. I've never topped it since: it was a real heart-breaker. The copy gives G7 as the chord in the second bar, but most times – and in the tenth bar, too – I was substituting a D minor seven with a flattened fifth, only I was playing the second inversion, with an A flat in the root. You should try it. It really darkens the tune up. Then in the middle eight, instead of those augmented B flats, I was putting straight A flat major sevens – and once I even tried a minor ninth, which I hadn't even thought of before then (fortunately I was able to communicate the news to my right hand just in time). I stretched it for six choruses, playing quiet to start with but really hitting the keys, really thickening the chords by the end. For the final chord I went down to C minor, and my last note – I can remember it now – was an A natural, right at the top. I've tried it since, and it didn't sound as good. It sounded just right at the time.

There was silence at first, then she started clapping, and then she came over to the piano. I turned around and faced her. We were both smiling.

'Thank you,' she said. 'That was beautiful. I've never heard it played like that before.'

I couldn't think of anything to say.

'My father used to love that tune,' she continued. 'He used to have a record of it. I used to listen to it a lot, but . . . you played it very differently. And you'd really never played it before?'

I laughed modestly. 'Well, it's amazing what you can do. When the inspiration's right.'

She blushed.

After a couple more numbers the manager came over and told me that I might as well go home. Nothing was said about coming back to play the next week. He gave me my cash and then went over to start closing up the bar.

'Oh well,' she said, '*I* enjoyed it. So would a lot more people if they'd been here.'

I finished packing my music away into a plastic bag

and said: 'Do you mind if I walk you home?' She looked hesitant. 'I don't mean anything funny. I only mean as far as your door.'

'All right, that's very kind. Thank you.'

And so that was as far as I got that evening – to her door. It turned out to be quite a door, all the same. About twice my height, at a modest estimate. It seemed to lead into some kind of mansion: one of those impossibly massive and gorgeous-looking Georgian houses you find in Onslow Square and those sorts of areas.

'You live here?' I said, craning my neck to look up at the top storey.

'Yes.'

'On your own?'

'No, I share it with another person.'

I tutted. 'That must be awfully cramped.'

'I don't own it or anything,' she said, laughing.

'You rent it? Really? How much a week? – Round it down to the nearest thousand if you like.'

'I work here,' she said. 'It belongs to this old lady. I look after her.'

It was a warm early summer's evening. We were standing on the pavement opposite the house. Behind us was a tall laurel hedge, and behind that, a small private park. Above us was the silver light of a street lamp. I leant against the lamp post and she stood quite close beside me.

'She's just a frail old lady. Most of the day she sleeps. Twice a day I have to take her up a meal – I don't have to cook it, there's a cook to do that. I can't cook. I have to get her out of bed in the morning, and get her into bed at night. In the afternoon I have to take her up a cup of tea and some biscuits and cakes, but sometimes she doesn't wake up for long enough to have them. I have to do her shopping for her, and go to the bank, and things like that.'

'And what do you get for doing all this?'

'I get some money, and I get some rooms of my own. There, those are my rooms.' She pointed up at two enormous windows on the second floor. 'Most of the time I don't have to do anything. I just sit up there, all day sometimes.'

'Don't you get lonely?'

'There's a telephone, and a television.'

I shook my head. 'It sounds, well, very different to the life I lead. Very different.'

'You must tell me about it.'

'Yes, I must. Perhaps,' I ventured, 'perhaps some other time?'

'I have to go inside now,' she said, and she crossed the road hurriedly.

I followed her and she unlocked the front door with a Yale key which looked absurdly small and puny for the task. There were three steps up to the door: I was standing on the second, and she was on the third, which made her seem quite a lot taller than me. When the door opened, I glimpsed a dark hallway. Madeline disappeared for a moment – I could hear the click of her heels on what

34

seemed to be a marble floor – and then the light was switched on.

'Jesus Christ . . .' I said.

While I was peering in, not even bothering to hide my awe and astonishment, she was picking up an envelope which must have been posted by hand through the letterbox. She opened it and read the letter.

'It's a note from Piers,' she said. 'He came round after all. How stupid of him.'

I was standing there like some idiot, not saying anything.

'Well,' said Madeline, 'this is as far as you go.' She started to turn away. 'Good night.'

'Look – ' Forgetting myself, I had laid my hand on her arm. Her grey eyes looked at me, questioning. 'I'd like to see you again.'

'Do you have a pen?'

I had a cheap plastic biro in my jacket pocket. She took it and wrote down a telephone number on the front of the envelope, beneath the word 'Madeline' which had been put there by her friend. Then she handed it to me.

'Here. You can phone me. Any time you like – day or night. I don't mind.'

And after saying that, she closed the door gently in my face.

*

Samson's wasn't very crowded – the weather must have been keeping people away – and we had the choice of whether to sit in the eating part or the drinking part.

'Are you hungry?' I asked. 'Or do you just want to drink?'

'I don't mind.'

I sighed.

'Well, have you eaten tonight?'

'No.'

'Then you must be hungry.'

'Not really. Don't you want to sit next to your friend?'

The piano was in the drinking area, but it was close to the open door of the restaurant, so that diners could still listen to the music. Tony was playing with his back to us and hadn't noticed our arrival yet.

'It doesn't matter where we sit,' I said.

'I thought that was the whole point of us coming.'

'We came because it's a nice place to come to. I didn't even know if he was going to be here.'

I must have raised my voice, because Tony heard me, turned round and waved with his left hand, while the other hand kept an attractive little arpeggio going on F sharp minor.

'Let's go through,' I said, indicating the restaurant.

'I don't want to sit and watch you eat,' said Madeline.

'You don't want anything?'

'Not particularly.'

'Well why didn't you say so? Fine, OK, we'll just have a drink.'

'But you're hungry.'

'For Christ's sake.'

I sat down at the nearest table and began looking through the wine list.

She sat beside me and said as she slid out of her coat, 'You are difficult, William.'

A tune went through my mind:

> There were times when I could have murdered her
> But I would hate anything to happen to her . . .
> I know, I know, it's serious

'Hello, young lovers,' said Tony.

We had started on the wine, a nice cold bottle of Frascati, and now he was standing over us, beaming down, waiting for an invitation.

'Got a few minutes to spare?' I asked, waving him to a seat.

'Thanks.'

We asked for a third glass.

'Nice version,' I said.

'You mean the Cole Porter? Yes, I thought I'd try it in a different key. Never done it in A before. It makes it sound sunnier, somehow. So,' he poured himself a generous glassful, 'how's everything going?'

I'd hoped he might begin by talking to Madeline, but his question was obviously directed at me, and I could tell that we were going to embark on a conversation about music from which she would be excluded.

'Well, we haven't rehearsed much recently,' I said.

'Tomorrow will be the first time in over a week. We've been recovering from the last gig. It was a bit rough.'

'Yes, you mentioned something about that.'

'I had a word with Chester about it. He was very apologetic, said he wouldn't book us into a place like that again.'

'So how's Martin? Have the bandages come off yet?'

'Yes, a couple of days ago, apparently. He can nearly hold his guitar again now.'

'Nasty.'

'Well, you know, you learn by experience. Now we know never to play at a place where the wine waiter has got "Love" and "Hate" tattooed on his knuckles.'

Tony smiled an accusing smile, as though at the scoring of yet another point in a long-running argument.

'Well, that's rock music for you, isn't it? Nothing like that has ever happened at a gig I've played at. And have you managed to practise any real music in the meantime?'

'I've been having a go at some of the ones you wrote out for me. I was meaning to ask you – I think you made a copying mistake somewhere. Three bars from the end of "All the Things You Are" – you meant B flat minor, didn't you, not major?'

'That's right. It's just a straight two-five-one. Why, did I write major?'

Madeline got up and said, 'Will you excuse me a moment? The ladies' is downstairs, isn't it?'

'Sure.'

Tony and I sat in a rather embarrassed silence for a while.

'I think she feels left out, when we start talking about music,' I explained. 'Perhaps we should try to keep the conversation more general.'

'Isn't it a problem?'

'How do you mean?'

'I mean going out with someone who isn't interested in what you do.'

'She's interested. Madeline enjoys music, all sorts of music. Like, she listens to church music a lot, especially.'

'Well, she would.' Tony poured me some more wine. 'So you're still getting on OK, are you, you two?'

Perhaps I should explain at this point that I'd known Tony for several years. In fact he was my first ever piano teacher. When I was back up in Leeds, doing the chemistry degree that I dropped out of, he was doing his PhD and earning some extra money by giving jazz piano classes. He had a small family to support even then: his wife, Judith, and their little son Ben, who was only five at the time. I got to meet them both soon enough, because I started going back for private lessons. They had a small terraced house in the Roundhay area, a really nice place with a piano and a garden and even a bit of a view towards the country, so that half the pleasure of going there used to be to see the family and maybe join in with their supper afterwards. Judith seemed to like having me as a guest, I could never quite fathom why. For some reason I never took to student life – all those sad men cooking up Pot

Noodles for themselves in shabby communal kitchens, taking them back to their rooms and eating them in front of *Dr Who* on a portable black and white TV – and I used to relish these quiet family evenings round at Tony's, with their good food and bottles of red wine, and Monk or Ben Webster or Mingus or someone playing away in the background.

That only lasted for my first year, anyway. Judith wanted to come to London where there was more chance of getting a full-time job, so the whole family moved down to Shadwell, taking Tony's unfinished thesis with them. Fortunately, through his involvement with the scene in Leeds, he had got to know some musicians here and soon found himself in demand as a teacher and performer. And it meant that when I (in my wisdom) decided that London was the only place for aspiring musicians to be, and gave up the losing battle with my degree, at least there was someone for me to anchor myself to. They had been very helpful. I owed a lot to them. It turned out that Judith's sister Tina was looking for someone to share her flat: she had this council flat in Bermondsey, a two-bedroomed place. I moved in there almost at once, and I suppose by and large the arrangement worked out – but I can talk about Tina later, because she was involved with what happened, too.

Neither Judith nor Tony hated London as much as I hated London, but he still hated it more than she did. Temperamentally he had always been dour and down to earth, with a tendency to look on the dark side and a genuine dislike of pretentiousness and affectation. He had a short well-trimmed black beard and darting intelligent eyes. He enjoyed making fun of people without their noticing, a form of humour I've never understood, and I was always slightly nervous about introducing him to people because the fact that they were friends of mine was no guarantee that he'd be polite to them. I'd begun to suspect that he didn't like Madeline very much. Not that he would ever have said so – not to me, at any rate – but I could detect this tiny antagonism. They had very little in common, you see, and there was also a certain simplicity about Madeline, a certain naivety, which I think Tony found grating. Perhaps he thought she was putting it on. This was behind his crack about her liking religious music: he was very suspicious about that side of her, he wouldn't buy it, whereas as far as I was concerned, it was one of the most attractive things about her. It was an unobtrusive, good-natured sort of religion, which showed itself in a general willingness to be kind and to think the best of people (not that much of this ever came my way). I remembered the last time we had come to Samson's, and Tony was talking about his father who had died a couple of years ago.

'I'm so sorry,' Madeline had said. 'How awful, to lose a parent like that, so early.'

'It doesn't make much sense, does it? The randomness of it.'

'But you know – ' and here she had actually touched his hand, while I looked on admiringly ' – the important thing is to die with dignity. Death can be gentle, and calm, and even beautiful. And if we leave this life with dignity, what is there to regret?'

'That's very true,' said Tony.

'How did your father die?'

'Gangrene of the scrotum.'

So Tony wasn't the best person to confide in about my relationship with Madeline, but then who else did I have? When it came to their emotional politics, the other members of the band were – and this is putting it kindly – unsophisticated. And after well over a year in London, I'd made hardly any other friends. Doesn't that speak volumes about this city? I lived in embarrassing physical proximity to my neighbours on the estate; I could hear them through the walls, throwing crockery around and beating each other up, but I never got to know their names. I could stand with my body pressed up against another man's on a crowded tube, and our eyes would never meet. I could go into the same grocer's three times a week and never have a proper conversation with the girl on the till. What a stupid place. But I mustn't lose the point. The point is that I was glad of Tony's question, glad of the chance to talk about Madeline while she was away.

'Yes, we're still getting on OK,' I said. 'No worse than usual, anyway.'

'Have you slept with her yet?'

It was no real business of his, of course, but I didn't resent the question.

'We think it's important not to rush things.'

'Well, nobody could accuse you of doing that. I should try and catch her before the menopause, all the same.'

'Anyway, you know, she has this Catholic thing . . .'

'Don't you find it frustrating?'

'I try to work it out in other ways. I think I'm using music as a substitute for sex.'

'Really? Well that's the last time you play my piano without washing your hands. Have you spoken to her about it? Do you talk about these things?'

'I'm waiting for the right moment to come up.'

'But it's been six months, William. And it can't be cheap, dating a girl like Madeline. Where did you take her tonight?'

I told him.

'You did *what*?'

'It was her idea. She's been wanting to see it for ages.'

'How much did you pay for the tickets?'

I told him.

'You paid *what*? William, you can't afford to do things like that.'

'I've been working lots of overtime. I can afford it, just, once in a while. Anyway, I've written to some magazines, and I think . . . I think it's only a matter of time before one of them gives me some work. I sent some sample reviews, and a CV. I spoke to this guy on the telephone, and he sounded quite encouraging.'

'Journalists are full of shit. How many times do I have

to tell you that? I mean, maybe, maybe you'll be lucky but you can't rely on any of these people.'

'Well, sooner or later I've got to get some kind of career for myself or I think I'm going to go nuts. I can't work in that shop for much longer.'

'William, you're young. Relax, carry on as you are, get plenty of practice in. You're a gifted performer, I've told you that, there's no saying what kind of break may come your way if you just stick at it. There's no reason on earth why you need to think in terms of a career at the moment.'

'Well, supposing I wanted to get married.'

'Married, at your age? You're kidding. Who would you marry?'

I raised my eyebrows and poured some more wine. Tony shook his head.

'I'm sorry, William, I don't think that would be a good idea.'

'*You* like being married, don't you? Having a home, and a kid and all that.'

'Yes, but you have to be ready for it. For God's sake, you've already been engaged once, and what are you – twenty-three? Cool off a bit. Just because you like seeing a woman now and again, it doesn't mean you have to spend the rest of your life with her. Think casual.' He looked at his watch. 'I've got to start playing again, I've had my twenty minutes.'

'Fine. We'll stay around and listen for a while.'

'Look, you've reminded me about something – could you do me a favour?'

'What is it?'

'It's about Ben. I was wondering if you were doing anything on the eleventh. A fortnight on Sunday.'

'I doubt it. Why?'

'Judith's boss has asked her up to some lunch party in Cambridge and she wants me to go along with her, but it's not really the kind of thing we can take Ben to. I was wondering if you'd mind sitting with him for the day. I'm sure we'll be back before the evening.'

'Sounds fine.'

I liked the idea of a day round at Tony's house: it would give me the chance to use his piano.

'Keep it free, then, will you? I appreciate it.' Tony stood up and stretched his fingers. 'Any requests?'

In the distance on the other side of the room I could see Madeline returning from the ladies'.

'How about "I Got it Bad and That Ain't Good"?'

He followed my gaze and smiled.

'Coming up.'

What did Madeline and I talk about for the rest of that evening? As I look back on the times we spent together, I find it almost impossible to remember the substance of our conversations. The awful suspicion raises itself that we spent most of the time in silence, or in conversation so banal that I have purposely blotted it from my memory. I know we didn't argue again that night, and I know that we didn't talk about the show. Perhaps we really didn't hang around for any longer than it took to finish off the remains of the wine. The next thing I can remember for sure is that we were standing in the depths of Tottenham Court Road tube, at the point where the paths to our different lines diverged, and I was holding her and stretching up to kiss her forehead.

'Well, good night,' I said.

'Thanks for taking me. I'm sorry you didn't enjoy it more.'

I shrugged, and asked, 'When can I see you again?' Suddenly the pain of being away from her was imminent, and as raw as it had ever been.

She shrugged too.

'How about . . .' I chose a day at random, at what seemed like a reasonable distance ' . . . Tuesday?'

'Fine.'

(She would have said the same if I had suggested meeting tomorrow or in six months' time.)

We fixed up a time and place, and then kissed good night. It wasn't a bad kiss. It lasted about four or five seconds, and our lips were slightly parted. It surpassed my expectations, in fact.

I wasn't exactly elated as I rode home, though. I took a Northern Line train down to Embankment and then joined the Circle Line eastbound to Tower Hill. It was the last train, I think. It was certainly well after midnight as I came out into the open air and began the thirty-minute walk back to the flat. The man on the ticket barrier recognized me and nodded tiredly and didn't ask to see my ticket. I turned up at this station and at this time so regularly that he probably thought I worked on a late shift somewhere. Tower Hill. It suddenly struck me as an appropriate title for a piano piece I was in the process of writing. It was meant to have a weary and melancholy feel to it – like you feel at the end of a long day, with maybe the vague hope of better to come. The first couple of phrases had emerged quite spontaneously in the course of an improvisation, and I'd been doodling with it for more than a week now, trying to put a structure on it. Perhaps having a title would help.

When I got back to the flat I went straight into my bedroom, switched on the keyboard and the amp and played what I'd written so far:

That was as far as I'd got. I'd had some ideas for the middle section but wasn't in a position to start working on them yet. What should come next? The C seven implied an F minor, that was easy enough; and suddenly, with a stronger idea in my mind of the mood I was striving for, I wrote the next four bars straight off:

I played all eight bars through, several times, and felt pleased with them; but still I couldn't think of a way to get the middle eight started. I tried thirteen different chords and none of them sounded right, so I gave up. I went into the kitchen to make myself a cup of tea instead.

Theme Two

loud, loutish lover, treat her kindly
(although she needs you
more than she loves you)

MORRISSEY,
I Know It's Over

While I was waiting for the kettle to boil, I looked to see if Tina had written me a note before going out to work. She worked on the night shift in the word-processing department of a big legal firm in the City; her hours were from seven in the evening until two in the morning. This meant that she was never in when I got home at night, and always asleep when I left for work in the mornings. In other words, we never saw each other. I doubt if I had seen Tina for more than two or three hours in total since moving into her flat. Even at weekends she would sleep during the day and stay up all night, and besides, I made a point of trying not to be in the flat at weekends, because

I found it too depressing. Just about everything I knew about her, then, I had learnt either from Tony and Judith, or from the notes which she used to leave me before going out to work. I knew, for instance, that she was about five years older than me and that she was dating a Spanish guy called Pedro, who lived in Hackney and worked similar hours to hers, as a mini-cab driver. She'd given him a key to the flat and he used to come in every morning at about three, just to sleep with her. Actually I don't know why I'd got the impression that he was smarmy. I'd never met him or anything. Until that night, I'd never even heard his voice.

For the purpose of leaving notes to each other, there was a pad of lined A4 on the kitchen table. It seemed so much more satisfactory than just writing on little scraps of paper. This way we could get a proper dialogue going. I picked up the most recent sheet and read over the whole of the last week's exchanges. They started fairly modestly, with a message from Tina:

Dear W, I see you have still not done the washing up. Nearly all the dirty crocks are yours and I'm blowed if I'm going to do it all for you. How do you expect me to cook a nice breakfast for P in the afternoons when I can't even get at the sink? A man phoned for you this afternoon. Love T.

T – The simple reason I have not done the washing up is that there is NO LIQUID, and I know for a fact it is your turn to buy it. Have you noticed those damp patches on the bathroom walls and what do you think we should do about it? Telling me 'a man phoned' is no use at all if you're not going to tell me what it was about. Did he have a Welsh accent? W.

Dear W, Are you blind or something, I put the washing-up liquid in the cupboard, right next to the chocolate biscuits. I'm sorry about the patches on the bathroom walls, it's nothing serious. P and I had a bath together yesterday afternoon and he got a bit excited, that's all. He's such a sweetheart. I'm not very good at accents – it sounded more West Country to me. Somebody else rang today only I'm not sure if it was the same person, they got me out of bed and I wasn't really with it. Are you going to eat up that cheese or just let it go mouldy? Love, T.

T – I've done most of the washing up, you'll notice, but didn't have time to finish it because I overslept. Why did I oversleep? Because the bloody phone woke me at four in the morning, that's why! I suppose it was good old Tommy the Toreador again. You didn't exactly keep your voice down while you were talking to him, either. You must have been nattering away for nearly half an hour. Incidentally could you take proper messages in future because these people ringing up for me might be offering WORK. Yes, I am going to eat the cheese. It looks in perfectly good condition to me. W.

Dear W, How do you think I felt, having to ANSWER the phone at four in the morning? I was devastated when P rang at that hour. He's never done anything like this to me before. He didn't give any proper reason for not coming over but I could hear music playing in the background so he must have been at some club or party or something. We weren't talking for NEARLY half an hour. In fact he was very short with me. And I had to raise my voice because he could hardly hear me. Anyway, I was damn well going to have my say, if he was going to treat me like that. I'm sorry if I disturbed your sleep but what about MY FEELINGS? I didn't sleep a WINK that night, as you can imagine.

I've thrown away your cheese. It was starting to pong the place out. Love, T.

P.S. What with your messages and P phoning up at all hours, what would you say to sharing the cost of an answering machine?

T – I'm sorry if Pedro upset you and you had a rough night, but I think it's a bit small-minded to take it out on an inoffensive bit of cheese. The kitchen still smells and if you look in the fridge I think you'll find that the culprit is your jar of taramasalata which is well past its 'best before' date. Yes, getting an answering machine would be an excellent idea and I'd be very happy to pay half. W.

Dear W, I had another bad night last night and I must

say it didn't help hearing you clattering about this
morning like a herd of merording buffaloes. Could you
not be a bit quieter when you get your breakfast in the
mornings? There have been no more calls for you but I
wonder if our phone is out of order or something
because I'm sure P would have rung up to apologize for
not coming round again. Have you got any intention
of giving me any money for the rent? It's been more than
four weeks now and I'm not made of money you know.
By the way I saw you out of the window today going
off to work and you do look thin. Are you eating
enough? There is some cold casserole in the fridge and
you are welcome to it. I made enough for two this
afternoon but guess who never turned up to have his
share.

I popped into Town this afternoon and bought the
machine. Exciting, isn't it? I hope I've set it up right. You
can check and also see if anybody has left a message yet.
Love, T.

I opened the fridge and found the cold casserole dish.
It looked pretty grim by now but tasted all right. I suppose
I should have heated it up and put it on a plate and
everything but that's not the kind of thing you feel like
doing at that time in the morning. I just got a spoon and
took the whole thing through into the sitting-room.

The answering machine was all fixed up and there was
a little green light flashing. I gathered from the instruction
book (which Tina had left by the side of the telephone)

that this meant there was a message waiting. I wondered if it would be my mysterious caller with the West Country accent, or maybe someone from *Midi Mania* magazine, calling to say that they'd read my reviews and wanted me to write for them. But as it turned out there was only one message, delivered by a voice which was unmistakably Spanish:

'Hello, Tina, my sweetest darling. Yes, it is Pedro, Big Boy, your little prickly cactus, and I was hoping to catch you before you went to work. Never mind. I was going to send you a million flowers to apologize for not seeing you again last night, but why don't I just come round tonight instead for a bit of a bath, and maybe something else, if you get what I'm drifting at. I know I can rely on you baby, to keep a light burning in your window. See you later, honeychops.'

The machine clicked off.

I scraped the rest of the casserole into the pedal bin. It was time for bed.

*

The estate I lived on was called the Herbert Estate. It was built in the 1930s, and I'm told there were even some of the original tenants there – people who'd been living on the estate for more than fifty years. Me, I'd been there about fifteen months and I couldn't wait to get shot of the place. It wasn't that I disliked my neighbours, it was just that I didn't feel I had much in common with them.

The standard uniform for men involved tattoos on the chest and forearms, and preferably a couple of Alsatians or Rottweilers on the end of a leash. The women just carried babies around with them all day – pushing them along in prams, or pulling them along in harnesses, or just walking to the shops with a whole crowd of little kids running around at their heels, shouting and screaming and making trouble. To keep these kids quiet their mothers would buy them sweets and crisps and chocolate and cans of sweet Coke and lemonade, which was why their complexions were so pale and their lips so red and their teeth already blackening. The women on the estate always seemed to be pregnant. There were six kids at least in the flat underneath ours and another one was on its way (by accident, as I was able to gather one night from a particularly loud argument which went on in the room beneath my bedroom). A lot of the men were out of work, and couldn't find much to do all day besides wandering around and visiting the pubs and the betting shop, so it's hard to see how these families made ends meet.

It wasn't an especially violent estate, it was even held together by a downbeat sort of community spirit, a shared sense that life was an uphill struggle and that as long as we were all living there, there was nothing to get too cheerful about. Every so often at night police cars would come tearing up with their lights flashing and their sirens wailing and there would be some kind of disturbance, but we would never find out what it was about. We had three locks on our door and bars on our windows so we never got broken into. Just up the road there was the Salvation Army hostel, and we used to get the drop-outs and winos walking up and down all day, going up to the park if the weather was good, or otherwise just dropping into the off-licence for their cider or their Special Brew, and then sitting down and drinking it out on the street.

It was a far cry from what I expected when I moved down to London. Then again, I don't know what I did expect. I'd had a nicely cosseted middle-class upbringing on the outskirts of Sheffield, and I spent the first twenty years of my life there without knowing enough about the world to realize how lucky I was. We were a close-knit family, the three of us, and I didn't make many friends: there was really only Derek, who lived next door, and Stacey, who I nearly married.

Derek was a couple of years older than me, but this had never seemed to make much difference, even during that teenage period when two years can seem like the most uncrossable of generation gaps. I suppose what kept us together was that we were both obsessed with music (although in different ways). My obsession tended to be practical: I was interested in listening to records purely for what I could learn from them and then apply to my own playing. (I was playing guitar at the time; I didn't move on to piano until I was nearly seventeen.) But Derek aspired to nothing more than consumption. He was avaricious about new trends in music, and would devour and digest them before the rest of us knew what was happening. It began with punk, which excited something in him even at the age of fourteen. At the time I was still listening to stupid bands who specialized in classical rip-offs and concept albums with great big gatefold sleeves covered with pictures straight out of Tolkien; but he soon talked me out of that. I used to go up to his bedroom and he'd play me the latest singles (I never used to buy singles) on his ancient Dansette record-player. He'd be buying five or six a week, maybe more. This was in the days when twelve-inch singles and picture discs were big news. Then there was New Romanticism (so-called), then there was a wilderness period when he went around looking gloomy and saying that there was nothing interesting happening, and then there was Hip-Hop and House to keep him happy. Meanwhile I had started playing in a local band and he would come dutifully along to our gigs, never saying much about the music, from which I guessed that he didn't like it particularly. Sometimes he would say things like we didn't have enough presence, and he'd criticize our haircuts. I suppose by then our friendship had developed in different ways and we didn't talk about music so often. I've always thought that the committed listener and the committed performer don't, in the long run, have all that much in common.

It was good that Derek used to come to our gigs, though, because he was company for Stacey. The two of them would turn up wherever we were playing – usually it was nothing more glamorous than a Saturday-evening support slot at the Leadmill – and stand in the front row where I could see them, and then the three of us would go along for a drink somewhere afterwards. Stacey was terrific. I still think this, even now.

At first when I left school I didn't want to go to college, I wanted to go straight into music, and the only job I could find which made use of my chemistry 'A' level was making up prescriptions behind the counter at Boots. That was where I met Stacey. She worked on cosmetics.

Why am I telling you all this anyway? I don't know how I got started on this subject. Everything has its place, and I'm supposed to be describing the Herbert Estate. And the reason I was doing that is because the next morning, at eight o'clock, I came out of the flat and started to walk through it on my way to work.

Progress was slow, to say the least, because I had my synth with me, and the combined weight of this keyboard and its carrying case was just about as much as my arms could bear. We would be rehearsing straight after work that night and I wouldn't have time to come back to the flat, so I had no option but to carry this monstrous thing with me all the way to the shop.

Out on the estate the first thing I saw was a bunch of kids, who should all have been on their way to school, throwing bricks at a bicycle. They all had skinhead haircuts and stonewashed jeans, and they jeered and shouted obscenities at me as I struggled past with my keyboard.

'What a wimp!' they were chanting.

I couldn't really disagree with them: they all looked about ten times stronger than me. On this estate I had once seen two eight-year-old children lift up a concrete bollard and hurl it through the window of a Ford Fiesta.

As I staggered past the grocer's and the chip shop I realized that there was no way I could carry the keyboard for more than another ten yards. I had been walking for five minutes and I had another mile and a quarter to go to the tube station. My face was purple, I was sweating profusely and I was gasping for breath. I dropped the keyboard on the ground, sat down on it and buried my head in my hands. After a while I tried to pick it up again. I couldn't. It was as if it was glued to the pavement. I sat down again and rested. One of my neighbours, several months pregnant, pushing a pram and with a small child in a harness on her back, came past and offered to carry it for me for a while. I politely refused. There was a call-box nearby: I knew I was going to have to phone for a mini-cab.

It was a dismal morning, misty and wet, and I sat on the pavement shivering and rubbing my hands as I waited for the cab to arrive. Ten minutes later an old beige Rover 2000 pulled up beside me.

'Cheapside, wasn't it?' said the driver, a tough-looking customer wearing an off-white vest that revealed an indecent pelt of hair adorning his back and shoulders.

'That's right,' I said, getting up.

He looked at my keyboard.

'Is that yours?'

'Yes.'

'Can't take that, mate. No way.'

'What?'

'You should have told them you wanted an estate or something. There's no way I'm taking that thing. No fucking way.'

'I'm sure it would fit on the back seat.'

'The back seat's for passengers, mate. This is a passenger vehicle, not a fucking removal van. Do you know what that would do to my upholstery?'

'Maybe if we tried the boot – '

'Have a look at that upholstery. Go on, have a look.'

I opened the back door and looked inside.

'Very nice.'

'Do you know how much that cost me? Sixty quid. Sixty quid, that cost me. If you think I'm going to fuck that up with heavy objects, you've got another think coming, mate.'

'Well, I see your point – '

'Should have cost twice that, of course, but this mate of mine, see, he did it cheap. Anyway, I could be sacked if I start doing removals. More than my job's worth, that is.'

'OK, look, forget it.'

'Six quid minimum, it'll cost you, if I'm going to take that big fucker in the back of my car. Where was it you wanted to go, Cheapside? Well, that's the other side of the river, isn't it, that's another fiver just to start with.'

'Don't worry, I'll get there some other way.'

'*I'm* not worried mate. *I'm* not worried. You're the one

that should be worried. 'Course, I shall have to charge you three fifty just for calling me out. If you'd told the bloke on the phone you wanted the contents of your house removing you could have saved us all a lot of trouble. What are you going to do now, then, catch a bus?'

'Yes, I suppose so.'

'Nearest bus-stop's half a mile away, isn't it? Anyway, no driver's going to let you on with that thing, are they? You know what I think, mate? I think you're well and truly fucked. Have you got one of our cards?'

He gave me a card with the name of the firm and a telephone number on it, and then drove off.

I don't know how I did it, but I staggered into work and arrived three-quarters of an hour late. Nobody said anything.

It was a tedious job, working in a record shop right in the heart of the City. The guys who came in to buy their Michael Jackson and Whitney Houston albums all looked like overpaid schoolboys. Not one of them seemed to have a spark of individuality. They all bought the same records and all wore the same clothes – striped shirts and fancy ties and smooth dark suits. I won't say anything more about this job except that I did it for about nine months and was always on the look-out for something better. For several months now I had been trying to get work with various music magazines: *Focus On Feedback*, *Midi Mania*, that sort of thing. Just doing reviews and so on. But it was impossible ever to get a straight answer from those people. God knows how many hours I spent on the telephone, being bounced from extension to extension: 'Could you hold the line, please?' 'Hang on, I'll just transfer you.' 'Line's engaged, can you hold?' And then nothing but equivocation: Yes, we've read your material. We'll get back to you in a few more weeks. We're keeping you on file. I've passed you on to Features. We'll let you know as soon as the right subject comes up. We're always interested in new writers. We're just waiting for Vivien to come back from holiday.

Some people don't realize that a straight 'No' can be the kindest answer in the world.

*

The band I was in at this time, which was called The Alaska Factory, used to rehearse at Thorn Bird Studios near London Bridge.

It was a big complex, occupying most of a converted warehouse which backed on to the river. There were six rehearsal rooms, Studios A–F, and two recording studios, Rooms 1 and 2, which were 16-track and 8-track respectively. There was also a refreshment area, where you could buy drinks and sandwiches, and a TV and a couple of games machines. The rehearsal rooms were damp and dark and used to smell something awful after you'd been in them for a while. Most of the equipment was clapped out and knackered. The only reason we went there, I suppose, was habit, and the fact that it was quite cheap.

Chester had worked out some deal with the guy who ran it, although how he'd managed to do that I don't know: I'd seen them talking together sometimes – often in a rather secretive way – and I gathered that they had some kind of understanding, based on God knows what shady arrangement. I didn't like to ask too much where those two were concerned. Anyway, we were just thankful not to have to negotiate a rate ourselves, because this guy was not, in our experience, the easiest person to get on with. I'll qualify that. He was a total slimeball.

I don't know if you've ever met anyone like this, but there are some people who are just so compulsively unpleasant that even when they desperately need your goodwill and your money, even when their very livelihood depends upon them being nice to you, they can't bring themselves to do it. Personally I think this is the mark of the true psychopath. I've never known anyone be so rude to his customers as this guy was. It wasn't just us, either. He did it to everybody.

He was a stringy sort of guy, probably in his late thirties but prematurely balding. All day long he would sit behind his desk, buttonholing any luckless musician who happened to pass by on his way from a rehearsal room to the lavatory and boring him to death with endless stories about his days on the road with any number of famous bands that he'd probably never had anything to do with. If he was to be believed, he'd been a drummer, guitarist, record producer and tour manager in his time, and fantastically successful at all of them. His name was Vincent, and just about the only work he ever seemed to do was to operate the till and unlock the doors to the studios and storage rooms. Sometimes, with a stream of sarcastic and patronizing remarks, he would guide people back to their rehearsal rooms, because it was incredibly easy to get lost in that building. It was an almighty labyrinth, taking up at least three or four floors (including the basement) of the old warehouse. I used to get lost there myself, looking for the lavatory or something, and I'd been going there for months. And it was amazing how, when you were wandering around in some unlit corridor – not even knowing whether to go up or down, there were so many little staircases – he would loom up out of the darkness with some stupid phrase like, 'Having trouble, are we?' and make a big deal out of taking you back to your studio. It was almost as if he kept tabs on where everyone was and what they were doing.

Initially, that evening, I thought I'd caught him in a good mood. This was a relief, because I was the first person to arrive, so I had to sit chatting with him for a while, while I waited for the others to show up. I began by asking what room Chester had booked for us that evening.

'Studio D,' he said. 'Three mikes and a Gretsch kit. That's right, isn't it?'

'Yes. I don't think we've been in there before, have we? It'll be interesting to see how it sounds; we weren't too happy with the sound we were getting in Studio E.'

I immediately realized that I'd said the wrong thing.

'What do you mean?' he said.

'It was . . . distorting a bit.'

'Distorting? Studio E? You've got to be joking, mate.'

'The sound was a bit . . . muddy.'

'Muddy? I can't believe I'm hearing this. That's the best fucking PA we've got, mate, it's brand new, that is, if you can't get a good sound out of that you must be fucking useless.'

'Well, it just sounded . . .'

'What was distorting, then? Vocals, was it?'

'Well, it was mainly the bass sound – '

'The bass? What's that got to do with the PA? What kind of amp was he using?'

'He doesn't use an amp, he goes straight into the desk.'

'Straight into the desk? Are you out of your fucking mind? That's a vocal PA, that is, mate, you can't put a bass through there. Was he using a D. I. box?'

'What?'

'Was he using a D. I. box?'

'Well, I'm not sure. I'm only the keyboard player, you see.'

He sighed contemptuously. 'You know what a D. I. box *is*, don't you?'

'Of course I do,' I said, with a nervous laugh. He started laughing, too, and we chuckled mirthlessly over the naivety of the question.

'Well he wouldn't try to put a bass through a vocal PA without a D. I. box, would he?' he said, and before I had time to answer, went on, 'In which case I can only assume that when you tell me that the sound you were getting was "muddy", you must be taking the old wee-wee. It's fucking immaculate, that PA. You've got a Yamaha REV-7 in the outboard rack for your vocal reverb, and a Roland SDE-3000 to give you short delay. You've got four dbx 160X compressors and two 27-band Klark Tekniks. You know what those are, don't you?'

'Sure. They're the . . .'

' . . . the graphic equalizers, right.'

'27-band, eh? Wow.'

'The whole rig's powered by C Audio amps, right? It's a four-way system with Brook Siren crossovers. They've all got compression drivers and there's even an extra cab with a 24-inch sub-woofer. So how the fuck can you be getting a muddy sound out of that lot?'

'Beats me,' I said, smiling desperately. 'Perhaps we forgot to switch it on.'

He ignored this remark.

'Anyway, you guys must have tried just about every bloody room we've got.'

'Not quite,' I said. 'We've never used Studio B.' I got up and walked over to his desk, so that I could see the diary in which he recorded all his bookings. 'Maybe we should try Studio B. Is anyone using it tonight?'

'Probably,' he said. 'It's very popular, Studio B.'

I tried to look at the diary but he suddenly leant over it, hiding it from view.

'Why does Chester never book us into Studio B?' I asked. 'What's so special about it?'

'We've been kitting it out,' he said. 'Putting a new PA in. It's not quite ready yet.'

I can't deny that I had been intrigued by this question for some time. Somewhere in the building – I'm not sure where – was a heavy black door with a big capital B on it. So far as I knew, no band had ever been allowed to use this room, and Vincent was always coming up with contradictory stories about why it wasn't available. Sometimes it was booked up for the next three weeks, sometimes it was being re-fitted, sometimes it was being used for storage. Sometimes he would give elaborate accounts of the new equipment he was installing there; other times, he would go tight-lipped at the very mention of it.

'We're not taking any more bookings for Studio B at the moment,' he said, snapping the diary shut. 'You'll be the first to know when we are.'

I was about to question him further, when we were interrupted by the arrival of Harry, our bass player and lead vocalist. The next few minutes were taken up with getting our instruments out of storage, testing the mikes and starting to set up.

We were in the smallest of the studios, and the one with the lowest roof. Harry, in fact, could barely stand up straight. I can't think of much to tell you about Harry, except that he was about the most normal and easy-going member of the band. He was an averagely good bass player and an averagely good singer. He played because he enjoyed it, and didn't have any great ambitions to be a pop star, or any difficult personal hang-ups. This was where he differed from the other two, who arrived together, about ten minutes later.

Martin was an insurance clerk by day and a guitar hero by night. He earned about four times as much as the rest of us (not that this is saying much), and everything he could save out of his income was spent on musical equipment. He had a hand-carved guitar and he would change the strings before every rehearsal. Sometimes he would change them between numbers. His amplifier, which was taller than he was, was worth more than the rest of our equipment put together. It had an absurd control panel which was a blaze of coloured lights and digital displays, and it was kept permanently in store because the four of us were incapable of carrying it anywhere. Lambeth Council could have re-housed half a dozen disadvantaged families in it. All of which would have been fine, if Martin had been a good guitarist; but the fact was that he only knew about five chords and had never managed to improvise a solo in his life. What he lacked in musical ability he made up in technical perfectionism. At one of our gigs, it had once taken him thirty-seven minutes to tune up. He kept us all permanently on a knife-edge because it only needed some tiny, barely detectable flaw in the sound we were getting for him to explode into one of his tantrums. Once, when we were playing in a pub in Leytonstone and had some feedback problems with the vocals, he stormed off stage and was later found to have locked himself in the boot of his car. He had crew-cut hair and an intense expression and he always wore a tie. I never saw him without one.

Then there was our drummer, Jake, a hardline existentialist with a black beret and gold-rimmed National Health glasses. Jake was still a student, doing a part-time degree in philosophy and literature at Birkbeck, I think. He practised in his room by using a copy of *Being and Nothingness* as a snare and all three volumes of *A la Recherche du Temps Perdu* as tom-toms. Like Martin, he had his limitations as a musician. He had a huge collection of records featuring some of the most technically adventurous drummers in history – Art Blakey, Elvin Jones, Tony Williams, Jack DeJohnette – but we never managed to teach him to play in any time signature other than 4/4, and he could hardly stray away from the bass drum and the snare without getting hopelessly confused. In fact this was the only drum pattern he knew:

Ask Jake to accompany you on a featherweight version of 'The Girl From Ipanema' and that's the pattern he would have used, at top volume. He used to write songs for the band, too, but we never bothered to play any of them. Somehow his twin passions for metaphysics and pop music never cohered into a satisfactory whole. He would end up writing songs which combined the philosophical complexity of 'Bat Out Of Hell' with the raw rock'n'roll energy of Schopenhauer's *The World As Will and Representation*. I liked Jake, on the whole, but found him infuriating. If he hadn't been so intelligent I think he would have been one of the stupidest people I ever met in my life.

It was the first time we had all met up since our last, disastrous gig, so before starting to play we sat around for a while and chatted about it. Morale was low in The Alaska Factory, at this time. We'd been playing live for nearly a year now, and it was beginning to feel as though we hadn't made an inch of progress. We still had the same hard-core following of about nine people, consisting mainly of relatives and girlfriends. (Madeline, incidentally, had never been to hear us play: in fact she had never even heard one of our tapes. She had never expressed any curiosity, and I didn't feel strongly enough about our material – most of which was written by either Harry or Martin – to make her listen to any of it. For my part, I never talked about Madeline to the rest of the band. They knew her name and knew that she was my girlfriend, but they had never met her, and I was happy to keep it that way. It satisfied something in me to be leading two completely independent lives. I knew, too, that she wouldn't have liked them; she wouldn't have liked the tattiness of Thorn Bird Studios, either, or the places where we used to eat afterwards, or the venues where Chester used to arrange for us to play.) Our hold on the pathetically simple music we used to play remained as fragile as ever.

It still wasn't unknown for us to lose time completely in the middle of a twelve-bar blues. And the thing that we were all holding out for, that mirage, the holy grail which is the gleam in the eye of every aspiring band – a recording contract – seemed, as usual, to be utterly beyond our reach.

This evening, moreover, we had business to discuss, because we'd decided that we were going to record a new demo tape. We'd each arranged to take time off work and we'd booked into Room 2 for Tuesday morning, in four days' time. Unusually, and largely because I had the support of Chester, I'd managed to persuade the others that we should record one of my pieces, an uplifting, danceable sort of number called 'Stranger in a Foreign Land' which was one of the latest things I'd written (Harry had helped me with the words). It called for one or two modest key changes and some shifts in dynamics that I wasn't sure we would be able to handle, so we agreed to spend most of that night's session practising it.

I gave Martin a chord sheet that I'd written out during my lunch break, and then turned to Jake.

'I think – er – I think we want to give this a kind of Afro-Latin feel,' I explained. 'You know, lots of off-beats.'

'Uh-huh,' he said, nervously.

I looked to Harry for support.

'Isn't that right?'

He nodded. 'Yeah, it's . . .' He begun to tap his feet and count silently to himself. 'It wants to go, sort of . . .

*chu*gga chugga chugga chugga chugga chugga chugga chugga, *chu*gga chugga chugga chugga chugga chugga chugga chugga. Isn't that the sort of thing?'

I frowned. 'Well, I was thinking more in terms of . . . chugga*chug* chugga*chug* chugga*chug* chugga*chug* . . . You know, as if we had shakers or something.'

'Well, why doesn't Jake try those out, and see which fits?'

Jake looked at us, from one to the other, nodded, spat on his hands, picked up his heaviest sticks and launched straight into:

After a few bars I signalled to him to stop but he was enjoying himself too much, and before I could do anything Martin had joined in, hammering out the same two chords incessantly so that the whole thing started to sound like a grotesque parody of a Status Quo number.

'All right, all right!' I shouted and waved my arms and managed to get them to stop. 'That sounded . . . just great, boys, but do you think we could get back to my song?'

'That was your song,' said Martin.

'It was?'

'Those are the chords you've written here.' He showed me the chord sheet. 'E and F sharp, right?'

'Well . . . nearly, Martin, nearly. You see, what we actually have here is an E minor nine, and an F sharp minor seven. You were playing major chords.'

'Does it make much difference?'

'Well, technically – yes. You see, they have different notes in them.'

'I think we should keep things simple.'

'Simplicity's great, Martin, I'm all for simplicity. Don't get me wrong. It's just that what you were playing, from a – well, from a musical point of view, really – is completely different from what I wrote.'

He didn't seem pleased by this criticism, and to express his annoyance he said, 'I think I'd better tune up again.'

Knowing that this would take some time, I left him to it, and went to find the lavatory.

It was either on the first floor or the second floor – after you'd gone across all those little landings, and up and down so many stairs, it was impossible to be sure – and when I came to find my way back to our studio, I got lost again. Just as I thought I knew where I was going, the lights went off (they were on some kind of time switch) and I had to grope my way along a pitch black corridor. At the end of the corridor, I found myself up against a locked door. It was very quiet. I was about to turn back, when I suddenly thought that I had heard a voice. I could have sworn that I heard a voice shout something behind the door – but as if from a distance. I could tell that the voice (which was male) was shouting quite loud, although the noise was heavily muffled by the door. Then again, perhaps I was imagining it. I stood there for a few seconds, straining to hear more, and then a hand gripped my shoulder. At the same time, the lights came back on, and I found that I was standing outside the door to Studio B, with Vincent's face pushed up close to mine.

'Oy, Rumpelstiltsken!' he said. 'What the fuck do you think you're doing?'

'I was lost,' I said.

'Get away from there, will you? Your room's bloody miles away. Come on, follow me.'

He tried the studio door, to make sure it was still locked, then led me away.

'Sorry about this,' I said. 'It's just that it's hard to find your way around this place sometimes.'

'You've been here often enough,' he said; but he seemed to be making an effort to let his anger subside. 'Anyway, how's it going tonight? Getting plenty done, are you?'

'We're rehearsing this piece for Tuesday,' I explained. 'You know, that session you're going to produce for us?'

The reminder seemed to cause him no particular pleasure. We weren't keen on the thought of a whole day in the studio with Vincent, either, but he came with the price of the session, and none of us knew how to operate an 8-track desk ourselves. At least he was experienced, if his own stories were to be believed.

I rejoined the others and for the next couple of hours concentration was high and the rehearsal went fairly well. I forgot about the voices I thought I had heard behind the locked door of Studio B. By ten o'clock, 'Stranger in a Foreign Land' seemed to be shaping up nicely, and Harry was just about getting the hang of the rather wide-ranging vocal line, when all of a sudden Martin screamed 'STOP!' at the top of his voice, threw down his guitar, and stood there with his hands on his hips, listening intently. We watched him in fear.

'Where's that hiss coming from?' he asked eventually.

'What hiss?'

'I can't hear any hiss.'

'The speakers are hissing. Can't you hear it? It's deafening!'

We listened for a while and then Harry said, in a conciliatory way, 'Well, it's not as if we need a perfect sound right now, this is only a rehearsal – '

Martin stamped his foot and said, 'God, this band is so technologically . . . illiterate! You're all such bloody – ' Then he stiffened again. 'What's that crackle?'

'What crackle?'

'I didn't hear any crackle.'

'Sorry, that was me,' said Jake, who had opened a packet of crisps.

Harry made the mistake of laughing.

'Right! That's it!' Martin shouted, and started unplugging his guitar and packing it away. 'I don't see why I should go on playing with a bunch of amateurs, who don't even realize the importance of having a good sound. It's like banging your head against a wall, playing in this band. There's no professionalism, no commitment . . .'

He picked up his guitar case, made for the exit, and said, before departing and slamming the door, 'Once and for all: I *quit*.'

He was gone, and there was a short silence. Then Jake put down his sticks, and began to take the drum kit apart.

'Well, there we go,' he sighed. 'Another hour of studio time down the drain.'

None of us were unduly worried, because this was at least the fifteenth time that Martin had threatened to leave. Usually he would just turn up at the next rehearsal without saying anything about it. It wasn't worth chasing after him: Harry lit up a cigarette, and I played through a few choruses of 'Autumn Leaves'. The atmosphere in the studio was tired rather than tense.

'Chester phoned up,' Harry said, after a while.

I stopped playing.

'Yes?'

'He thinks it would be a good idea if we all got together and had a talk.'

'Fine.'

'Sunday lunchtime, at The White Goat.'

'Fine.'

'I'll call Martin and tell him, shall I?'

Harry and Jake decided to go to the kebab shop, but I couldn't face it. I got a bus back from Borough High Street and managed to persuade the driver to let me bring the keyboard on. The bus only took me to within half a mile of the flat, so I had to walk the rest of the way; with a few pauses for sitting down and getting my breath back,

I was able to do it in about twenty minutes. I didn't even meet any winos or kids this time, although there seemed to be some kind of trouble going on in the chip shop. These two blokes had got the owner up against the wall. It looked as if they were trying to rob the till or something. I didn't feel like getting involved.

I arrived back at the flat and was about to turn the television on, thinking that there might be an Open University programme worth watching, when I noticed that the green light was flashing on our answering machine. There were no messages for me, though. It was Pedro again.

'Hola, Tina, it's only me, ringing to find out how are you feeling, my little dumpling. You know, you shouldn't have upset me by crying like that and calling me names, especially names like that which I'm surprised to be known to a lady of your persuasion. Anyway, I hope you're feeling better and I suppose I'm sorry about what happened last night, I suppose I got a little bit carried off, and I hope I didn't hurt you or things like that. You know, in Spain, men and women, we do things like this all the time, but maybe you English ladies are a bit less uninhabited. Anyway, I'll come around tonight again, if you still want to see me, and maybe we can pick things up where we got off. OK?'

There was a long pause.

'I'm sorry.'

The machine clicked off.

Middle Eight

Were you and he Lovers?
and would you say so if you were?

MORRISSEY,
Alsatian Cousin

Nobody, absolutely nobody who had any real choice in the matter, would choose to spend Sunday morning on a council estate in South East London. Waking up in the morning and staring at the damp patch in the ceiling of your bedroom, a brief vision passes through your mind of all the beautiful places in the world, all the different places where you could have found yourself, and you realize that somebody, somewhere, has seriously miscalculated. The sun is shining. It's a fine, crisp, wintry morning. You have two options. You can either lie in bed all day, and try to forget where you are, or you can get up, and get out – it doesn't matter where, just some place that doesn't make you feel quite so suicidally depressed. All over the estate, people must be thinking these thoughts; in every single flat, there must be people planning their escape. You'd have thought, wouldn't you, that there would be a mass exodus from the Herbert Estate every Sunday morning, that the streets would be thronged with desperate men, women and children making a concerted bid for freedom. But it doesn't happen. Nobody moves. Everybody stays put. Do you know why?

Because there are no fucking buses, that's why.

It's not that there aren't meant to be buses, of course. Somewhere, perhaps hidden away in some long-forgotten vault or archive, there must be a timetable telling you when and where these buses are supposed to run. There is even a little panel on the side of the bus-stop, where this timetable is supposed to be posted, although the timetable itself is never there. I think London Transport employs vandals specifically to tear down its timetables within seconds of putting them up, so that people have no idea when the buses are meant to run and can't complain about them never appearing. Standing at a bus-stop on a Sunday morning is like going to church: it's an act of faith, an expression of irrational belief in something which you dearly want to believe exists, even though you have never seen it with your own eyes.

At first you are the only person at the bus-stop. You have allowed several hours for your journey and you feel stupidly optimistic. You whistle a tune. Twenty minutes go by, and then a bus comes, but it's out of service. Never mind, these are early days yet. An old man joins you at the bus-stop, and asks you if you have been waiting long. You say, about twenty minutes. He nods and lights up a cigarette. You begin to make anagrams out of the words in the advertisements posted up on the other side of the road. You count all the windows in the block of flats to your right. Another twenty minutes go by, and you are beginning to grow impatient. Your foot has started tapping. The old man has finished his cigarette, given up and disappeared. Your legs are beginning to ache, and you shift your weight from one to the other restlessly. Just behind you is a little shop, and the owner, a Cypriot, is standing in the doorway looking at you with this infuriating beatific, knowing smile on his face. He is smiling because he knows – and so do you, although you dare not articulate it to yourself – that your ordeal has barely started yet.

More time passes. You have stopped whistling and you've run out of anagrams. You keep looking at your watch: so often, that you know the time it is going to tell you almost to the very second. More people join you at the bus-stop. Some of them give up after a few minutes, and walk on. By now, however hard you try to fight against it, hollow, tearful despair is beginning to well up inside you. An old, old woman goes past, muttering to herself and pulling a little trolley full of dirty washing. You hate her. You hate her because you know that you will be seeing her again. Even though she is walking at the rate of a mile a century, you know that she will have time to go down to the launderette, do three loads of washing, call in on her sister for Sunday lunch, eat the whole meal, wash up, watch the omnibus edition of *EastEnders* and walk all the way back before the next bus comes. You start thinking of all the things you could have done in the time you have been waiting for this bus. You start adding up all the hours in your life spent waiting for buses that never came. The whole, sorry history of mankind, the entire catalogue of human suffering and misery, seems suddenly crystallized in this futile activity. It makes you want to cry.

By now quite a crowd has gathered at the bus-stop. People are sitting on the pavement, shivering, with their heads in their hands; women are breast-feeding their babies; small children are wailing and moaning and running around in distracted circles. It's like a scene from a refugee camp. And you are also incredibly hungry. The little Cypriot shop behind you is still open, and you wonder whether you should perform an act of charity, because it is within your power to put all these people out of their misery. Because you know that if you step inside that shop, just for thirty seconds, to buy a bar of chocolate, a bus will immediately come around the corner, and it will have gone again by the time you get outside. There is absolutely no doubt in your mind about this. But at the same time you can't help wondering if it might be worth taking the risk: given that the bus will appear, not immediately when you enter the shop, but at the precise moment when you hand over your money to the shopkeeper – mightn't there still be time for you to collect the change, run outside and leap on the bus? It's worth a try. So you go inside, and you choose a bar of chocolate, and the Cypriot shopkeeper has gone to lunch and left his eight-year-old son to look after the till, and you hand over a fifty-pence piece, and glance anxiously out of the window, and the bus has come, and the little Cypriot boy is scratching his head because he doesn't have the faintest idea how to subtract twenty-four from fifty, and you shout 'Twenty-six! Twenty-six!', and he opens the till but there are no ten- or twenty-pence pieces, and he slowly begins counting the whole thing out in coppers, and you look out of the window and see that the last person is just getting on to the bus, and you shout, 'Forget it, kid, forget it!', and run outside just as the bus is pulling away, and the driver sees you but he doesn't stop for you, because he's a complete and utter bastard.

What follows is a short burst of hysterical laughter, and then the descent of a strange, immutable calm. It seems deathly quiet after the crowd of people has got on the bus, and there is no longer any traffic of any description on the roads. You look at your watch but it means nothing to you because you have now entered upon a different plane of temporal consciousness in which normal earthly time has no meaning. You feel serene and content. You begin to feel that the arrival of another bus would be unwelcome, because it would break the spell of this new and lovely euphoria. The thought of spending the rest of your life at this bus-stop fills you with benign indifference.

Waiting here now seems to have been a rich and fulfilling experience because it has taught you a philosophical detachment which many greater men would envy. You are now master of an heroic fortitude which makes Sir Thomas More on the day of his execution look pathetic and petulant. Your Stoical composure makes Socrates, with the hemlock poised at his lips, look like some neurotic cry-baby. It feels as though nothing on earth has the power to harm you any more.

Just then, something comes around the corner, heading in your direction. It is a taxi, with its yellow light on. Not even bothering to check whether you can afford the fare, you hail it, and jump inside.

*

'Sorry I'm late,' I said, nodding apologetically to Chester. 'I had a bit of trouble catching a bus.'

Harry, Martin, Jake and Chester were all sitting around a small table near the bar. Nobody looked particularly cheerful. Jake had a book open on his lap.

'That's all right,' said Chester. 'No harm done.' He smiled at me, straightened his cap, and sipped his beer.

'I'll just go and get something to drink,' I said, 'since you've all got one.'

I was served at the bar by this woman who was fairly new to The White Goat. I'd only seen her two or three times before, and although on one of these occasions we'd had a bit of a chat, I wasn't sure that she'd remember me. She did, though. She had long, thick auburn hair and a Scottish accent, and her voice was gentle and quiet, like her eyes. I didn't like to admit it to myself, but I was very attracted to her. I couldn't work out what she was doing in a place like this, pulling drinks. She seemed abstracted half of the time, her mind on something completely different, and she didn't talk to most of the customers, which made it twice as odd that she had talked to me. Today I was determined to find out her name.

'It's me again,' I said, unable to think of a witty opening line.

'Oh, hello. Becks, isn't it?'

'That's right.' She fetched a bottle from the cold tray. 'Is there no band today, then?'

'You missed them. They only played for about forty minutes. They weren't very good.'

The White Goat had a policy of showcasing new bands on Sunday lunchtimes. The Alaska Factory had played there once, in fact. We had only played for forty minutes and we hadn't been very good. I was glad that this had been before her time.

'Are you a friend of Chester's?' she asked.

'That's right. Do you know him?'

'I'm getting to know him. He comes in here all the time. Very strange company he keeps, sometimes. All sorts of shady-looking characters.'

'Chester's our manager.'

'Oh? You're a musician, too?'

84

'Yes, I'm a pianist really.' I jerked my thumb in the direction of the others. 'We just do this for a laugh.'

'They don't seem to be laughing much,' she said, looking over at them.

'Well, we're going through a bit of a crisis right now. You know, stagnating, that sort of thing.'

'That's a shame.'

I shrugged. 'It's nothing that a few minor personnel changes wouldn't put right. We need a new guitarist, and a new drummer.' She handed me my drink. 'And probably a new singer, too.'

'Uh-huh.' Then she said, in an off-hand way, 'I sing a bit.'

'Really?'

'Well, I used to. I still do, now and again.'

'What sorts of things?'

'All sorts of things.'

'I see.' I watched her, increasingly fascinated, as she counted out my change. 'What's your name?'

'Karla. Karla with a K.'

'I'm William.'

'Hello, William.' She pressed the change into my hand.

'Are you singing with anyone at the moment? A band or anything?'

'No, nothing like that.'

I tried to imagine her singing. Perhaps she would have a breathy voice, redolent of smoke-filled cafés and sad, sensual ballads from the thirties and forties. Perhaps her voice would be bright and clear, like a Scottish stream, and she would sing folk songs and good, strong tunes from her native country.

'Where are you from?' I asked.

'I'm from Mull,' she said. 'Originally. We moved to the mainland when I was quite small, though. Haven't been back to the island in years.'

I took a breath and said, 'Look – maybe we should get together and do some songs some time.' These words sounded tacky even as I spoke them. 'I could accompany you.'

'I think your friends are getting impatient,' said Karla.

I followed her gaze and saw that they were all staring at us. Harry made a 'come here' gesture with his eyes. I went over to join them and Karla started serving another customer.

Chester said, 'Do you think you can spare us some of your time, or are you too busy chatting up women?'

'I was only getting myself a drink.'

'We've got some serious talking to do,' said Martin. He was the only person in the pub that afternoon to be wearing a tie.

'What about?'

'The band.'

'There seems to be a general consensus,' said Harry, 'that we've got ourselves into a bit of a rut.'

The whole business of sitting around a table and discussing something so trivial seemed suddenly ludicrous. There was an upright piano standing against one of the walls and I was seized by a powerful urge to go over and play something on it, just to get away from them all. But I stayed where I was.

'Chester's been saying,' Harry continued, 'that we need to do two things. One, we need to break on to vinyl. We've got to get a record company interested, so it's essential that we record a good demo on Tuesday.'

'Fine,' I said, yawning. I was thinking of how nice it would be to accompany Karla on a version of 'My Funny Valentine', leaving her to take care of the tune while I filled it out with rich harmonies, constantly surprising and pleasing her with unexpected changes and variations.

'Two,' said Harry, 'we've got to improve our stage act. The reason the audience was so aggressive last time is that we didn't have any authority. We didn't impose ourselves on them.'

'Come off it,' I said. 'The problem with last time was that we were playing to a crowd of psychos and drillerkillers. Hitler would have had trouble establishing authority with that lot.'

'All Harry's trying to say,' said Chester, 'is that you've got to think harder about how you present yourselves.'

There was a pause.

'And what does that mean, exactly?' I asked.

'Harry and I have been thinking,' said Martin, 'and we think you ought to stand up on stage.'

'What?'

'That stool you sit on when you're playing the keyboard,' said Harry. 'It's got to go.'

'I don't believe this,' I said. 'Our audience consists of

the London branch of the Myra Hindley fan club and you think they're going to be stunned into submission by the sight of me getting up from my chair?'

'We're not just talking about last time. It's a question of the whole . . . concept of the band.'

'It's about attitude,' said Martin, 'and dynamics.'

'Well forgive my naivety,' I said, 'but I always thought it was about music.'

'The music's fine,' said Martin. 'There's nothing wrong with the music. We're talking eye-levels here.'

'If I stand up, I can't use my pedals.'

'*We* both stand up,' said Harry, 'and we manage to use our pedals.'

'I'm sorry, this is just incredible to me. I mean, next you're going to be asking me to wear one of those keyboards around my neck, like I was selling ice-cream.'

'We just want you to stand up, that's all.'

'You think Vladimir Ashkenazy has to stand up when he's playing the Moonlight Sonata? To establish *his* authority?'

'That's different,' said Jake. 'A classical pianist establishes authority through a set of quite distinctive signs, such as the suit he wears, and the way he walks on to the stage and sits down. It's a question of semiotics.'

'Whose side are you on?' I asked.

'Yours, actually.'

The others looked at him in surprise.

'I think Bill should carry on sitting down. Otherwise it upsets the balance. At the moment we've got two people standing up and two people sitting down. That communicates poise, and equilibrium.'

'Fuck equilibrium,' said Martin. 'Think feet and inches.'

I stood up.

'This is completely ridiculous.'

'William, will you for God's sake sit down!' shouted Harry.

'I thought you wanted me to stand up.'

'I want you to stand up *now* and sit down on *stage*. I mean, I want you to sit down *now* and stand *up* on stage!'

'Cool it boys, will you?' said Chester. 'There's no point in losing our tempers.'

'Why don't you just get yourselves a taller keyboard player and be done with it?'

'We're not getting personal about this, Bill. We value your contribution to the band. You know that.'

I sighed. 'Does anybody want another drink?'

It turned out that everybody wanted another drink, except me: I had only asked because I wanted to go up to the bar and talk to Karla again. I wasn't even able to do that, because Chester and Harry insisted on sharing the next round. While they were away, rather than talking to the other two, I sat down at the piano. Much to my surprise, it was unlocked. There was no jukebox in the pub and the level of conversation was high enough for me to be able to play softly without anybody noticing.

I played through the first eight bars of 'Tower Hill' twice, and my finger rested on the last note, the high E flat. I still hadn't managed to get any further. But now some part of me remembered a harmony I had heard once – a minor seventh chord, with the melody starting a fourth above the root. In which case, E flat would give . . . B flat minor seven. I tried it. It sounded nice. A melodic figure came quite readily:

Harmonizing this was easy. All it needed in the second half of the bar was to flatten the fifth. It never ceases to delight me that you can alter a chord by just one semitone and produce a completely different effect like that. This figure would come to rest, of course, on a C natural, with an A flat major seven being held for the whole bar. That C natural also gave me the clue for the next development – a repeat of the previous two bars, only a minor third lower, and with a C seven substituted for the second chord. The pattern of the melody stayed broadly the same, too, so that the whole four-bar sequence now played like this:

I was beginning to feel pleased with this piece – not because it was in any way original, or because it was anything special technically, but because it was coming to express my feelings towards Madeline very clearly. I wondered if I should play it to her when it was finished, and explain that it was written with her in mind. Perhaps then she would understand the dissatisfactions I felt, the frustration and the longing to get closer.

But it was a long time since I had played the piano to Madeline. After our first meeting, when it had been music which brought us together, I had assumed that it would always be like that – that it would always be an area of shared understanding between us. As it turned out, I was being naive. When I started playing the piano at Mrs Gordon's house, the first time that Madeline allowed me to visit her there, she came running into the room and told me to stop in case it woke the old lady up. It was a lovely old Bechstein grand, too.

'What's the matter?' I said. 'Didn't you like what I was playing?'

'She's asleep. You'll wake her.'

It was early evening: the beginning of the end of a bright summer's day. I had come straight over from the record shop and the smell of the City was just starting to wash off. I couldn't believe my luck, to be spending the evening in such a nice part of town, with such a lovely woman, in such a beautiful house. There were huge oil paintings on the walls in every room – family portraits, Madeline told me – and heavy red velvet curtains and Regency furniture, and splendid marble fireplaces topped with gilt-framed mirrors. I had seen nothing like it since the days when my parents used to take me around stately homes.

'I've made some tea,' she said. 'Shall we go upstairs?'

She had a large, sunny room on the second floor, as well as a bathroom and a small kitchen all to herself. She served Earl Grey tea in bone china cups and didn't offer me milk or sugar. There was a television, a telephone, a hi-fi, a large single bed, a writing desk, a dressing-table and two high-backed but comfortable armchairs. The walls were decorated with nineteenth-century landscapes. It was a warm and friendly room but it said nothing about Madeline herself, except that she was obviously happy not to impose her own personality on to it. One slightly unexpected feature was that a small crucifix had been placed on top of the dressing-table.

'Is she religious, this woman?' I asked (meaning Mrs Gordon).

'No, not especially.' She saw what had prompted my question. 'That's mine.'

'I didn't know you were a Catholic.'

'Well how could you? You've barely met me.'

I sipped my tea, chastened, and said, 'I went through a brief religious phase once. I used to go to communion every week. Apart from anything else, it's still the only place you can get a drink first thing on a Sunday morning.'

She didn't laugh or even smile, and I felt that I had struck a wrong note.

'What would you like to do this evening?' she asked. 'Shall we go out somewhere?'

'Sure,' I said. 'Anywhere you like.'

We walked to a little Hungarian restaurant on the

Kings Road. I tried putting my arm around her waist on the way, but could feel no encouragement, so I withdrew it at the first opportunity. Not that she asked me to or anything. It was just a sense I had.

'What are your plans?' she asked me, after we had ordered our food.

'Pardon?' It seemed an odd question.

'What are you going to do? With all this music and everything. Where's it going to lead?'

'I don't know, I hadn't really thought. That's not why I'm doing it.'

'Why are you doing it?'

'Well, you know . . . I'm only twenty-three, after all. I've just got to make myself known, play as often as possible – there's no saying what might happen. I've got this friend, Tony, who used to teach me, and he thinks that I've got the potential – ' I couldn't think why I was telling her this, so I decided to stop. 'Anyway, what about you? How much longer are you going to look after Mrs Gordon?'

'What else can I do?'

'I don't know.'

Madeline paused, and then said another odd thing.

'My parents think I'm an accountant.'

'What?'

'After I left university, I started to train as an accountant. That was where I met Piers – you know, the friend I was supposed to be seeing that night? But I got bored, so I gave it up. But I haven't told my parents about it yet.'

'When was this?'

She frowned. 'Nearly a year ago, now.'

'Where are your parents?'

'In America. Daddy works for this bank. They asked him to be an overseas manager.'

'Don't you miss them?'

'No.'

'Do you have any brothers or sisters?'

'A brother. He's in Japan somewhere.'

'Do you miss him?'

'No.' She smiled, blandly. 'We weren't very close, my family. We travelled about all over the place. My parents went to Italy for a while and left us with relatives. They separated for a while and I lived in Ireland with my mother. It feels as though my father and I never spent more than a few months together.'

'So when did he use to listen to "My Funny Valentine"?'

The reference didn't seem to register.

'I've only had two phone calls from them in all the time they've been away. But every so often I write to them. That's when Piers is useful.'

'In what way?' I asked. For some reason I already disliked this Piers character. (Well, forget 'for some reason'. It was for the obvious reason.)

'He still works for this accountancy firm, you see, and he can get me sheets of their headed notepaper. So I write to my parents on this notepaper and they still think I'm working as an accountant.'

'That's awful,' I said. 'Why do you have to lie to them?'

'They'd be furious. They didn't put me through university just so I could end up as a glorified nanny.'

'My parents have never tried to stop me doing anything I wanted to do,' I said. 'They trust me.' I hope this didn't sound as pompous to her, then, as it does to me, now. But I could feel my mood deteriorating and I asked her another petulant question. 'So you and Piers are pretty close, are you, one way and another?'

'We're just old friends, that's all. I like him.' She held up her wrist. 'Look, he gave me this, once.'

'What, the bruise?'

'No, silly, the bracelet.'

It was thin and elegant and looked as though it was made of solid gold and had cost him about five thousand pounds. I hated it.

'Very nice,' I said. I would have to find out when her birthday was and start putting money into a savings account.

'Don't worry,' she said. 'He's not my boyfriend.'

I thought that if my feelings were that obvious, I might as well press the point.

'There've been . . . men in your life, have there?'

'Not really,' she said, seeming more bored than embarrassed by the question. 'There was someone a couple of years ago, but it wasn't very serious. We used to meet on Saturdays and go up to walk his dog on Hampstead Heath.'

'What was his name?'

'Rover, I think. This food's a long time coming, isn't it?'

I always have this problem with restaurants. I know that the idea is to catch the waiter's eye, or to make some kind of discreet gesture; there are some people (Chester would be one of them) who only have to make some lazy little movement with their right forefinger for a whole army of waiters to descend on them, dancing attendance. Me, I can get up and stand right in their path, waving my arms about like someone trying to flag down a speeding taxi, and they still manage to look right through me. I wouldn't mind, but this disability seems to rub off on to whoever I'm dining with: so there we were, the only two customers in this bloody restaurant, with about fifteen waiters standing over by the till acting like the place hadn't even opened yet.

'I suppose I only liked him,' Madeline said suddenly, 'because he was a Catholic.'

'It's that important to you?'

'It makes a difference.'

'I'm not a Catholic.'

'I know. I don't mind.'

I looked at her full in the face for as long as I thought good manners would allow. She was without doubt the most beautiful woman I had ever dated. Oh, Stacey was pretty, there's no denying that: but Madeline was in a different class altogether. It occurred to me, from the way she was dressed, from the way her hair was done, from the way she was made up, that she must have spent hours preparing for this evening, and I felt suddenly ashamed of my shabby work clothes and my sloppy assumption that I could just turn up at her house, without making any special effort, and expect the whole occasion to go swimmingly. A swirl of feelings, compounded of desire and incipient affection and a wish to apologize, swept over me and it was all I could do to refrain from leaning across the table and kissing her long and gently on the mouth.

When the time came to kiss her good night, in the lamplit doorway of that unbelievable mansion, I was determined to do the job properly. I don't know what expectations I had arrived with, exactly, that night. Somewhere at the back of my mind I had probably believed that I would end up sleeping with her, but there was no sense of frustration or anti-climax when I realized that this wouldn't happen, tonight or even for some time to come. I was happy, for now, to cup her cheeks between my palms, to feel her face tilt expectantly towards me, to plant my open mouth against hers, to sense a tiny yielding, and then to whisper 'Good night, Madeline' and hear her murmur in reply. As I walked back towards the tube station, I felt that no satisfaction could be more complete.

Perhaps I would have been less happy if I had known that on this first date, Madeline and I had come as physically close as we would ever come; that we would never surpass that kiss – wouldn't even equal it, more often that not. Except once. Except for an evening when we had eaten somewhere near the Aldwych, the Waldorf or some other place that I couldn't really afford, and we walked down to the Thames, and she slid her hand into mine, and one minute we were standing looking at the water and then the next she had put her arms around me and suddenly we were kissing with a passion which baffled and astonished me, her tongue crushing against mine, her mouth biting into my lips until it was me, after all, who had to withdraw and look away. She never explained those moments to me and after I had seen her on to her train, I staggered home across Waterloo Bridge like a drunken man, reeling with shock and pleasure, my head and body throbbing with excitement.

'Are you sure you won't have another?' somebody asked.

It was Chester, standing over me as I sat at the piano.

I closed the lid.

'Why not?' I said, and followed him to the bar.

Just as Chester was paying for my drink, a tall, angular, sallow young man rushed in and grabbed him by the shoulder. He had restless eyes and a shock of black hair, greased back and centre-parted, and he seemed very agitated. Chester registered surprise and, I thought, even a little anger on seeing him.

'Paisley? What the hell are you doing here?'

'I've got to talk to you, Chess. I need to have a word.' He didn't look at Chester as he said this, but kept staring restlessly around him, as though he thought he was being followed or something.

'Not now, Paisley, for God's sake. Can't you see I'm busy?'

'I just need a quick word. Five minutes.'

'I told you not to come and find me here, didn't I?'

'Five minutes, Chester.' He put his hand on his shoulder and started clawing it until Chester pushed him away.

'Piss off, can't you? I'll come and find you later.'

'Look, you don't understand. I don't just *want* a word. I *need* a word. I *need*, Chester, I need.'

He was looking into his eyes by now; but still his gaze was unsteady, darting uncontrollably.

Chester paused for a moment, tight-lipped, and then said, 'Christ, you're a pin-head, Paisley. You're a real fucking Christmas turkey. Come on, and make it quick. Excuse us a minute, Bill.'

They disappeared in the direction of the exit; or it could have been the Gents, I'm not sure. I was left standing alone at the bar. Just me, and Karla, drying glasses.

'Who was that?' I asked her.

'I don't know. I've seen him here before once or twice. I told you Chester knew a fairly strange crowd.' She smiled. 'I don't think you really know him very well, do you?'

'I don't know him at all.'

'You find out quite a lot about your customers, working behind a bar. In bits and pieces. I know all the regulars, now. Sometimes even when I'm not working I just stand at the window and watch them coming and going.'

'What window?'

'I live right opposite here, above the video shop. I can see everything that goes on at this place.'

'What is there to see?'

'You never know, do you?' She smiled again, and it was almost as if she was talking to herself. 'You never know who you're going to see.'

I could make no sense of this remark, so I used it as an excuse to change the subject.

'I'd love to hear you sing. Seriously. Maybe we could come in here one morning before opening time, and use the piano.'

She shook her head, laughing. 'That's the worst chat-up line I've ever heard in my life.'

I was indignant.

'It wasn't a chat-up line. Listen, I've got a girlfriend, you know. I'm not trying to chat you up.'

She took me more seriously once I'd told her that, but still all she'd say was, 'I said I *used* to sing, that's all. And I don't think you'd like my voice very much.'

Chester reappeared, looking breathless and apologetic.

'Sorry about that, Bill. Did you get your drink?'

'Yes, thanks.' I gestured at the other members of the band, who seemed to be in various stages of clinical depression. 'Do you think it's worth carrying on with this?'

He looked at his watch. 'No, we're wasting our time. See how the recording goes on Tuesday, eh? Maybe things'll look up when you've got a decent demo under your belts.'

'I'd better get back. The buses are completely fucked today, it'll probably take me hours.'

'You live over Rotherhithe way, don't you? I can give you a lift.'

'Really?'

'Yeah, I've got to see someone over there, about four o'clock. No problem.'

So it was that I found myself sitting for the first time in Chester's little orange Marina, speeding past the Angel and down through the City and out across London Bridge. And it was then, also for the first time, that he raised the subject of Paisley, and Paisley's band The Unfortunates – the band of which Chester was also the manager.

'I've been thinking about them, you see. Listening to their tapes, that sort of thing. The thing is, they need a keyboard player.'

'Oh?'

'You know, a real musician. To fill out the sound a bit. They've got real style, this band, they could really go somewhere, but musically they . . . well, they need a bit of help.'

I paused long enough for him to perform a particularly agonizing gear change.

'Is this in the nature of a . . . proposition?' I asked.

'Yes, you could say that. That's very well put, William. A proposition. Exactly.'

'Well, I . . .'

'You probably want to think about it.'

'Yes. Yes, I would.'

'Fine.'

He took me to within half a mile of the flat and then pulled up at a junction. He seemed worried that he was going to be late for his appointment.

'I'll drop you here, if you don't mind. This bloke, he gets a bit mad if you keep him waiting.'

'A bit mad?'

'Yes, you know. A little bit nasty.' And before I had time to wonder what he might have meant, he had straightened his cap and was driving off. The last thing he said to me, as he wound up the window, was: 'Think about it.'

Interlude

Panic on the streets of London . . .
I wonder to myself
Could life ever be sane again?

MORRISSEY,
Panic

So I thought about it. That is, I thought a lot about
Chester, and about Paisley, and the strange encounter I
had half-witnessed in the pub that afternoon. I thought
about it over the next week, and I thought about it on
that dreadful Saturday night, as I ran through the back
streets of Islington, each step taking me further and
further away from Paisley's smashed and lifeless body.

I must have run for about ten minutes without stopping.
Perhaps that doesn't sound like very much, but for
someone like me, who hasn't taken any proper exercise
for years – not since I was at school – believe me, it was
quite an achievement. I tried to keep some sort of sense
of direction at first, but soon I found myself in totally

unfamiliar territory. Looking now at the *A–Z*, I think I must have started off by heading west, towards Camden, but then a series of leftish turns must have taken me in the King's Cross direction. The first place I can remember stopping was a bus-shelter, and the first thing I can remember doing was forcing myself to think: forcing myself to look at the situation I was in and imagine how it would seem to an outsider.

I had been spotted at the scene of the crime. I had been seen by two policemen, emerging from the house where Paisley had been murdered. And instead of trying to explain myself, I had turned around and run, thereby immediately drawing suspicion on to myself. Well, perhaps when they caught up with me – which I was convinced they would – I could account for that, saying that I was in a state of shock and I didn't stop to think about what I was doing or how it would look. One or two other circumstances were in my favour: at least there wasn't a murder weapon with my fingerprints on it, for instance.

As for the killing itself, I was just about in a fit state to realize that there were two possible explanations. Either somebody, for some reason, had wanted to get rid of Paisley, or, more likely, they had mistaken him for someone else – the mysterious 'landlord' of the house where they all lived. Who was he, though? The only person who knew him, it seemed, was Chester himself, and he had been very unforthcoming about his identity. Deliberately unforthcoming, perhaps? Karla had told me that Chester had some strange friends. She had also pointed out to me that I didn't really know him very well. Had I been a little too trusting with our friendly, resourceful, enigmatic manager? What sort of hold did he have over Paisley that could give rise to a scene like the one I had witnessed in the pub that Sunday afternoon? Maybe Chester himself was the owner of their house – maybe he was the one the telephone callers kept asking for, under a succession of different names. Or perhaps I was on completely the wrong track: was Paisley the real target of the attack, and if so, could it have been Chester himself who was behind it?

As I sat in the shelter I saw that there was a bus approaching, and suddenly I decided to get on to it. There was no way the police could have issued a description of me yet, so it wasn't as if any of the passengers would recognize me. All the same, I paid my fare in cash, rather than showing the driver my travelcard with the passport photo on it. I jumped on without even looking at the front of the bus and without any idea of where it was going to take me. The important thing was that it took me away from here as soon as possible. I sat on the bottom deck, near the back, and willed the bus to move.

And then, of course, panting up to the bus-stop came the bane of every journey – the passenger who gets on at the last minute and doesn't have the faintest idea where he wants to go. Usually a tourist who can't speak much English and has decided to use the driver as a combination of policeman, street map, bus timetable and change machine. So the bus is stuck there for what seems like a million years while he names some street in Greenwich or Richmond where he wants to go, and the bus driver has to get out his *A–Z* and explain to him which stop to get off at and which bus he'll have to catch next, and then the bloke tries to find his fare and he only has a twenty-pound note or ninety-five pence in Japanese yen and the driver has to fish the change out of his back trouser pocket and you could have travelled to Glasgow and back on an inter-city sleeper by the time the bus starts moving again.

When we finally got going, I began to relax very slightly. The experience of being on a bus had a comforting familiarity and normality to it, so that the horrible thing I had witnessed less than twenty minutes ago began to seem almost absurd. The world I was in – the world of half-empty London buses on a Saturday evening, carrying young, smartly dressed people off to parties and clubs and cinemas – didn't seem to admit of anything as fantastic as the spectacle of two screeching dwarves bashing a man to death. It was stupid. It was crazy.

Stupid and crazy . . . and yet this was familiar, too. Dwarves and death. Why did it strike a chord – where had I come across these words recently? And then I remembered. It went back to a conversation we had had, the four of us, on the morning we recorded our demo tape.

Was this just coincidence, or had I actually stumbled upon a clue?

Solo

did I really walk all this way
just to hear you say

'oh I don't want to go out tonight'

MORRISSEY,
I Don't Owe You Anything

It had been a fine feeling to wake up on Tuesday morning
and know that I didn't have to go into work. Even though
we had to be at the studio for ten o'clock, this still meant
an extra hour in bed. There was no sound from Tina's
room. This was a relief, too. For the last few nights,
strange noises had been emerging from behind her door:
muffled cries and grunts, suggestive of physical exertions
which I preferred not to speculate about. The toilet kept
flushing as well. But I had been lying awake when she
came back in from work the night before, and it had
sounded as though she was on her own.

There were no notes for me in the kitchen. I took my

toast into the sitting-room, watched *Breakfast Time* with the sound turned down and decided to catch up on the latest messages on the answering machine. I had come back quite late myself last night and hadn't got around to listening to them yet.

There were four messages. One of them was from Madeline: she said that she couldn't see me tonight after all and could we make it Thursday instead? I was disappointed, of course, and also a little puzzled. She was always telling me that she had no social life apart from her evenings with me. Perhaps she was ill or something.

The other three messages were all from Pedro. They had each been left at different stages of the evening and together they made up quite a little narrative. The first one was relatively coherent and the only thing you could hear on it was his voice. He must have been calling from his flat.

'Hello, Tina, my little breast of chicken, my little piece of fur. Listen, I will be a bit later than my usual this evening because I am taking the night off and going with some friends to paint the town. But I will still come and see you because I couldn't do without you for a single night of my life. Expect to feel my key in your lock before dawn, then, my love. Adios.'

For the next message he was speaking from a call-box: he was slightly louder and there were some voices and some music in the background. His speech was starting to sound slurred.

'Hi, Teeny-babes, we're having a great time here, and I'm just ringing to say . . . Hope I can make it tonight . . . I still want to come . . . Maybe I'll be pretty late but I hope you'll still be wearing something nice like that thing I bought you. You know, that cost me a lot of money and it's not every shop that will sell you something like that, and I'm sure if you had another go at it you could fit – '

The pips went and the message ended.

The last one seemed to have been left a few hours later. This time the voices in the background were both male and female, and the music, although it was louder, was now slow and sensual.

'Hi, Tina, we're having quite a time here, we're all higher than a kite and it would be just great if you could come over and join us because we have some great people here, all really good friends of mine, and we could do some great things here if we had a girl like you here, so please come over and bring some things over with you because I . . .'

This time his voice was just cut off without any explanation, and the tape stopped with a click. He hadn't left an address for Tina to go and find him. Her door remained ominously shut.

★

Vincent was in a particularly cheerful mood when we arrived at the studio that morning. His favourite customers were using one of the rehearsal rooms: not us, of course, but an all-female band called The Vicious Circles. He was, I need hardly tell you, one of those typical music-business technicians who specialize in making the lives of female musicians a misery. When I arrived, one of The Vicious Circles was standing at his desk complaining that she couldn't get her amplifier to work.

'Do you think you could come and look at it?' she was saying.

'Look at it? I'll do more than come and look at it for you, darling. I'll bring my plug along and stick it in, if you like.'

He was wearing a T-shirt on which a picture of an enormous red rooster was accompanied by the words, 'Nothing like a nice big cock to wake you up in the morning'.

'Look, I'm only asking you to come and give me a hand.'

'Oh, I don't mind giving you a hand, darling. A hand'll do nicely to start with. Har, har, har!'

'I'll go and do it myself,' she said, turning.

'Anything else wrong, is there, darling? You wouldn't like me to have a look at your fuzz box, would you? Har, har, har!'

She was about to go back downstairs, when two small children suddenly appeared through the front door, wearing matching anoraks. Immediately, all Vincent's joviality evaporated and he stared at them in horror and fury. For several seconds he was speechless; then he exploded.

'Kids! What the fucking hell are two bloody kids doing in here? Get them out! Go on, piss off!'

The woman ran over to her children and gathered them in her arms reproachfully.

'Look, I thought I told you to stay in the car.'

'It's boring,' said the eldest.

'Are these yours?' Vincent asked.

'Yes.'

'This isn't a fucking kindergarten, you know. Who said you could bring your kids here?'

'Well what else am I supposed to do with them while we practise? I can't afford a minder.'

'Get those kids out of here and lock them in your fucking car, and don't bring them in here again.'

'Come on,' she said, taking them both by the hand. 'Back to the car. I'll keep coming out and seeing you, and I'll bring you some sweets.'

Vincent turned to me after they'd gone, apparently expecting to find me in sympathy with him.

'Women with kids should stay at home and look after the little fuckers,' he said. 'They don't know a tit from a tweeter anyway, this lot. Totally clueless.'

'How's Studio B coming along?' I asked, anxious to change the subject.

'Oh, you know, a bit of work still to do. You'll be the first to know when it's ready.'

'How long's it been out of action, now? Quite a few months, isn't it?'

'No, no, a few weeks, that's all.'

'That's funny, because whenever I talk to the other bands who use this place, none of them have ever been in there, either. It seems to have been shut for as long as we can remember.'

He put his face uncomfortably near mine and looked me squarely in the eye.

'Do you mind if I give you some advice, Bilbo?' he said. 'Don't ask so many questions. All right?'

I nodded.

'Come on then, we've got work to do.'

Jake and Harry were already waiting for us in the studio; Martin presumably knew that we wouldn't be needing him until later. Once inside the studio Vincent became quiet and efficient and began checking the mikes set up around the drum kit. Jake was looking nervous: he knew that his part was the first to be recorded, and that he'd have to get it right early on in the session. It wasn't a particularly complex drum part, though, and besides having a click track to keep him in time, I was going to provide a basic keyboard part so that he'd know where he was in the song.

As soon as he started playing, though, I could tell that he hadn't learnt the song properly. He had no real idea where the transitions were meant to come, and he was far too tentative about putting in fills. And, in spite of my pleas to the contrary, the pattern he was playing was a none-too-distant cousin of:

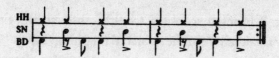

After six or seven takes he was basically no better, just a little more polished and relaxed, so I thought we might as well cut our losses. As Jake sweated his way through the fade-out, I gave a thumbs-up to Vincent on the other side of the glass, and Harry was sent through to put down the bass line.

We got an excellent take from Harry on his second go, by which time Martin had arrived. There followed a prolonged interval for re-stringing and tuning. Vincent gave him a brief lecture about the folly of putting new strings on just before a recording session, and I felt, for once, slightly grateful to the bad-tempered old bastard. Martin scowled and dithered over whether to use a thick or a thin plectrum. At first when he started playing, his chords seemed to bear no relation to the bass line: it transpired that he was playing them three frets too high. There was a minor seven which he kept playing as a major until it practically drove me mad with frustration. He attempted impossibly ambitious arpeggios where the song called for simple power chords. His B string kept going out of tune. By the time we had even a half-way decent take, it was getting on for one o'clock.

'We'll have to finish this this afternoon,' said Vincent, gleefully. 'It'll cost you double, of course.'

'You'll have to speak to Chester about that,' I said. Chester paid all our rehearsal and recording bills.

We went to the pub across the road, a square, detached, concrete building calculated to depress the most flighty of spirits. Martin bought a round and we sat drinking it in morose silence, conscious that the morning had gone just as badly as we had all expected.

'Catchy tune, that,' said Jake eventually, having hummed a few bars of 'Stranger in a Foreign Land'.

'Yeah,' said Harry. 'It's a nice one.'

I resented these limp attempts to cheer me up.

'Perhaps we should have recorded something a bit simpler,' I said.

'No, this is a good one to do,' said Harry. 'It's direct, it's tuneful.'

'Not exactly chart material, though, is it?' said Martin, sipping his beer and glowering. 'It's not what you'd call commercial.'

'That's such a bloody old-fashioned thing to say,' said Jake. 'That distinction just doesn't exist any more. Anything can get into the charts these days, absolutely anything, as long as it's properly marketed. That's why they're so full of shit.' He took a mouthful of Guinness and closed his eyes. 'God, I wish we were back in seventy-six.'

'Why, what happened in seventy-six?' asked Martin.

Jake eyed him up to see if he was being serious.

'You've heard of punk, have you?'

'Punk? That was never twelve years ago, was it?'

'It bloody was,' said Harry. 'Twelve years almost

exactly. "Anarchy in the UK", released November the twenty-sixth, nineteen seventy-six. What a band, eh? What a band.'

'The Damned, "New Rose". That came out then, too.'

'No, that was earlier, about a month earlier.'

'If you two are off wandering down Memory Lane again,' I said, 'I'm going to go for a walk or something.'

They ignored me. Once they got going on this subject, Jake and Harry (who had both been in their teens during the late seventies) were unstoppable.

'What about The Vibrators, eh? "We Vibrate".'

'The Jam. The Buzzcocks. The Adverts. Siouxsie.'

'May the seventh, nineteen seventy-seven. The London Rainbow. I was there. What a fucking brilliant night that was. The Clash, The Slits, The Jam and Subway Sect.'

'X-Ray Spex, "Oh Bondage Up Yours". Great single.'

'"Spiral Scratch".'

'"Pretty Vacant".'

'"Right to Work".'

'"Get a Grip".'

'Do you remember The Rezillos?'

'Do you remember Alternative TV?'

'Stiff Little Fingers.'

'The Desperate Bicycles.'

'XTC.'

'999.'

'Slaughter and the Dogs.'

'What about The Dwarves of Death?'

The flood of reminiscence stopped and Jake stared at Harry in surprise.

'Who?'

'The Dwarves of Death – they did that single, what was it called . . . "Black and Blue".'

'You're making this up.'

'No, you remember them, surely? I mean, it didn't chart or anything, but they were a real cult band.'

'I think you're pulling my leg.'

'No I'm not. They did two singles – "Black and Blue", and then another one, I can't remember the name.'

'Look, I was around at the time, right? I can remember the name of every band from the punk era. Stop taking the piss.'

'I'm not. Honest. You *must* remember. There were four of them – they had this amazing girl singer with a really unpleasant voice – made Poly Styrene sound like Kiri Te Kanawa – and they had this guitarist and this bass player who were both dwarves. Brothers. That's where they got the name.'

'That's only three,' I pointed out.

'Well, there was some other guy. The drummer or something.'

'Sorry, Harry, I'm not buying it.'

'Are you calling me a liar?'

'I just don't believe you, that's all.'

'Look, why don't we ask Vincent?' I said, thinking that we already had enough trouble on our hands without falling out over a stupid argument like this. 'He's always going on about how he was right there in the thick of it when punk happened. Ask him, he'd remember.'

And so it was Vincent who settled the argument, after a fashion, with a curt 'Nope, never heard of them', when we got back into the studio. Harry began to sulk and Jake grinned in triumph. Then shortly afterwards, he and Martin left: their jobs were done and there was little point in them hanging around to watch the tedious process of me and Harry finishing the song off.

We had recorded the drums in stereo, so now, with the drums and bass guitar all laid down, we only had four tracks left to complete the recording. We decided to put the vocal line down on one track and leave the other three free for keyboards. The real hook of the song was a recurring figure which should really have been played on the saxophone, but we didn't know any saxophone players so we had to make do with a fairly convincing sample which Vincent had found for us. I recorded that, and a piano part, and added some strings, and then Harry had a go at the vocals:

Now and then
I wonder if I should have come here
Real men
Who's going to ask me what I've done here?

I search for buried treasure
Precious gifts from out of Araby

> I know it's now or never
> And when I'm down, will you carry me?

I shook my head sadly as he sang these lines. I've always found it hard to write lyrics, and as Harry struggled to get the top B at the beginning of each phrase, these ones sounded more lame than ever. Then there was the chorus:

> And then I went away
> And I left behind the times
> And the place where she stayed
> Often lingers in my mind
> Wish I knew what you planned
> Feel your fingers in my hand
> I just hope I can stand –
> Stranger in a foreign land

By five o'clock the recording was finished. We took an hour off to have some tea, then came back to do the mixdown. We listened to the finished version a couple of times and tried to feel good about it.

'There you are, boys,' said Vincent, presenting us with a reel of one-inch tape in a white cardboard box. 'Your passport to success.'

'Sarcastic bastard,' said Harry, when he'd gone out of the room. He opened the box and looked at the tape. 'I suppose we'd better get a few cassettes and make some copies of this, had we?'

'Perhaps we'd better leave it a few days,' I said, 'and listen to it again.'

Harry must have sensed the pessimism that this implied. He nodded understandingly.

'I believe you,' I added. 'About that band.'

He shrugged.

'Doesn't matter really, does it?'

'Look, I've got this friend, back in Sheffield. He knows everything about music. He's a walking encyclopaedia. I'll write and ask him – he'll know.'

'It's no big deal. Really.'

But I could see that it mattered to him, and I decided to do something about it that evening. Besides, I had been out of touch with Derek for far too long.

*

The tune of 'Stranger in a Foreign Land' was still dancing around my head as I waited for Madeline outside the Swiss Centre in Leicester Square on Thursday evening. I suppose when I wrote those words, 'Wish I knew what you planned, Feel your fingers in my hand', she had been at the back of my mind – where she always was, when she wasn't at the front. The chords I had used were meant to have a bitter-sweet feel – alternating minor sevenths, a whole tone apart, a favourite mannerism of mine – but on the whole the piece was designed to sound optimistic and forward-looking, which was still how I tried to feel about the relationship: in the face, it has to be said, of much discouraging evidence.

And that evening, the evidence started to pile up. It started with her being late. This in itself was unusual: she had never kept me waiting for more than about five minutes before, but this time she was more than half an hour late, and it was past nine o'clock by the time I spotted her threading through the crowds from Piccadilly Circus.

'Sorry,' she said. 'My watch must be slow.'

'You aren't wearing a watch,' I pointed out.

Madeline pulled her coat tightly around herself.

'Don't snap at me when I've just arrived,' she said. 'What are we going to do, anyway?'

'I thought we could go to a film, but it's too late now, they've all started.' I expected her to apologize again at this point, but she didn't. 'So, I don't know . . . I suppose we might as well get something to eat.'

'Don't sound so enthusiastic.'

'It's just that I've hardly got any money.'

The sheer predictability of my feelings for Madeline never ceased to surprise me. Ebb and flow, ebb and flow. In her absence, a simple longing; as soon as we were together again, irritation, petulance, angry devotion. Whenever I saw her I was immediately struck by how beautiful she was, and then immediately devastated by the thought that I had known her for six months and still not even come close to making love to her. And yet, just when I was dying to give vent to my emotion, I was expected to be cool and level-headed, to look around me and to choose, from the hundreds of restaurants on offer in the Leicester Square area, the one where we were to go and have dinner. French? Italian? Greek? Indian? Chinese? Thai? Vietnamese? Indonesian? Malaysian? Vegetarian? Nepalese?

'How about going to McDonald's?' I said.

'Fine,' she said.

We went to the one on the Haymarket, and sat upstairs. I had a quarterpounder with cheese, regular fries and a large coke. All Madeline would have was a cheeseburger. We ate in silence for a while. She was clearly depressed about something and her moroseness didn't take long to spread in my direction. I thought of all the evenings we had spent together in the last six months, all the hope and excitement I had felt at the start of the relationship, and it seemed cruel and pathetic that we should be sitting there, not even talking, just picking at junk food in these bland surroundings on a freezing winter's night. When I finally dared to speak, it seemed to require enormous effort.

'So,' I said, 'what have you been up to, the last few days?'

'Nothing much. You know me.'

I pointed at her cheeseburger.

'Is that all you're going to eat?'

'I'm not very hungry. Anyway, I hate this food.'

I must have made some gesture of frustration, because she took pity and said: 'I'm sorry, William. We're both in a bad mood, that's all.'

I could have pointed out that I hadn't been in a bad mood, until she kept me waiting for half an hour, but it seemed more constructive to take her up on her attempt at friendliness.

'We recorded a new song on Tuesday,' I said.

'Oh?' Naturally, she sounded bored.

'Took us all day, in fact. Six hours' studio time.'

'This is turning into quite an expensive hobby, isn't it?'

'You know perfectly well it isn't a hobby.'

She took one of my fries and said, absently, 'You still think you're going to make a career out of this, do you?'

'I don't know. I really don't think of it in those terms.'

'Why do you do it then, this music? What's the point?'

'I do it because I have to.'

Her stare was blank, uncomprehending.

'I do it because I've got all this music, locked up inside me, and I have to let it out. It's . . . what I do. It's what I've always done.'

'Sounds most inconvenient: like a bowel problem or something. I'm glad I don't have it.'

'No, it's not like that at all. It's a gift. It's a way of expressing feelings – putting them into permanent form – preserving them. Feelings which would otherwise just be dead and forgotten.'

'What sort of feelings?'

Bravely, I said: 'Feelings about you, for instance.'

'You've written songs about me?'

'Yes.'

'How embarrassing.'

There was a short silence, during which I wondered whether she realized how wounding this had sounded. Then I said, 'Thanks.'

'What do you mean?' she asked – picking up on my sarcasm, for once.

'You know something that really pisses me off?'

'If you're just going to be rude to me tonight,' she said, 'I don't have to sit here and listen.'

'I'll tell you what pisses me off. It's how nice you are.'

'What?'

'How nice you are to everybody but me. God, you're so polite, and gentle, and considerate, and generous, you're so brimming over with good feelings for everyone: and not a scrap of it comes my way. Not a bloody trickle.'

'I think you're being unfair. Very unfair.'

'No I'm not. Why should you treat me differently from anyone else? Just because I'm your boyfriend, that doesn't mean I'm not entitled to a bit of courtesy now and again. Jesus, you keep me waiting for half an hour, you're sulky, you won't talk to me. You won't even tell me what's wrong.'

'There's nothing wrong.'

I took hold of her chin and forced her to look at me.

'Yes there is. Isn't there?'

She looked away.

'I don't want to talk about it.'

My fingers had been covered with pickle and tomato sauce. She took one of the paper serviettes and wiped her face clean.

I sighed. 'Tell me, will you? You owe it to me.'

She tried to meet my gaze but had to look away as she said, brokenly, 'I want . . . a change.'

'A change?'

'In this relationship.'

I frowned.

'What sort of change?'

'You *know* what sort,' she said, looking up again.

'No I don't.'

For several seconds we stared at each other, two pairs of eyes in angry, hopeless deadlock, straining to communicate and yet straining to block each other out. Finally Madeline broke away.

'God, you're stupid,' she said. 'I've never known anyone as stupid as you, William.' She stood up and put her bag over her shoulder. 'I'm going.'

'Going where?'

'Home.'

'Don't be silly.'

'I'm not being silly. I've had enough and I'm going home.'

'I'll come with you to the bus-stop.'

'Forget it. I don't want you to. I'd rather go on my own.'

I stood up, too.

'Will you stop messing around? Are we going to talk about this properly, like two – '

She pushed me back down into my seat.

'Shut up and finish that cheeseburger.'

And before I had time to stop her, she was off, running down the staircase and disappearing from view. I sat there, baffled. In front of me was a plastic carton containing a half-eaten cheeseburger: a potent symbol of a failed relationship if ever I saw one. After a few moments I pushed it into the waste-bin and left the restaurant myself.

There was no sign of Madeline out in the street. I knew which bus-stop she would be walking to, but there seemed no point in following her: better to let this mood subside, and maybe call her tomorrow. The evening was turning colder, and there was a damp mist in the air. I buttoned up my thin old raincoat, thrust my hands deep into the pockets, started to wander aimlessly up the street and then struck out in the direction of Samson's.

It was a long shot, but it paid off: Tony was there. I didn't want to speak to him right away, though, so I sat at a table in the corner and ordered a bottle of wine, which I began to drink on my own, slowly and methodically. The next thing I knew, it was three-quarters empty. The place was practically deserted, so there wasn't much in the way of distractions – conversation, clinking glasses, the scraping of chairs – to prevent me from listening to his piano-playing. We had 'Night and Day', 'Some Other Time', 'Blue in Green' and, finally, 'My Funny Valentine'. Though I say it myself, it wasn't as good as the version I had played for Madeline that night. It was more polished, but less emotional. It got to me, all the same, prompting me to wander over to the piano, before Tony had a chance to start his next number.

'Hi.' He seemed genuinely pleased to see me. 'What are you doing here?'

'When's your break?' I asked.

'Well, I could take one now.'

'Come and have a drink, then.'

We ordered another bottle of wine, even though he didn't seem to drink much of it, and I filled him in on the argument with Madeline. I don't know what I expected to gain from confiding in him in this way. Men don't tend to be a great deal of use to each other at times of emotional crisis, and I found myself wishing that there was some woman I could have gone to, someone who wouldn't have felt embarrassed about hugging me, to start with, and then discussing the whole thing openly. Tony, I could see, was also suffering from the temptation to say something along the lines of 'I told you so'. I wasn't going to let him do that.

'Well, I might as well try to forget it,' I said eventually.

'I think that's a good idea.'

'I've got other things to think about. Lots to get on with.'

'Exactly.'

'Besides, I can phone her in the morning.'

He looked at me, smiled and shook his head.

'You don't think you should leave it a bit longer than that?'

It occurred to me that what he was saying was something in the nature of a final break: a prospect which, as soon as I contemplated it, plunged me into fear and panic.

I had a momentary sensation of falling and weightlessness, like you get in a lift when it descends too quickly. I shivered.

'We'll see. I'll think about it.' To avoid discussing the matter further, I said: 'I've written a new piano piece.'

'Really?' said Tony. 'How does it go?'

I had indeed completed 'Tower Hill' only the previous evening. The last four bars of the middle eight had turned out to be rather complicated, involving further modulations and a more elaborate approach to the melody, but I liked them and felt that they fitted. I had got, you may remember, as far as an F major seven, held for a whole bar. Well, for the second half of that bar I had now added an F sharp diminished, with a little linking figure on top which went like this:

This now led into a G minor (picking up on the one two bars earlier), an unexpected B flat minor, and then on to a strong A flat major from which, by descending thirds, I quickly progressed to a D flat. From there an E flat seven was the obvious way to get back to the beginning of the piece, although it seemed to need a little help by having some extra harmony voiced in the right hand:

I liked the patterns of thirds in the penultimate bar of this section, and I liked the momentary sense of fullness in the fourth, as you poised on that last chord before returning to the main tune. But naturally, now that the piece was finished, it was open to interpretation in all sorts of different ways, and a performer was under no particular obligation to follow my voicings. I was already keen to hear what another pianist would make of it.

'Do you have any paper with you?' I asked Tony.

'Sure.'

He always carried a slim leather briefcase with him, full of song-copies. From this he now produced a sheet of blank manuscript paper which he handed to me, along with a pen. Within a few minutes I had written it out. I pushed it back across the table towards him and his dark, intelligent eyes scanned it keenly, picking out the highlights and constructing, in his mind, a sound-picture of the total effect.

'Very interesting,' he said. 'Quite nicely done, that.'

He tried to return it to me but I stopped him.

'Will you play it?'

'What, now?'

'Yes. I'd like to hear it.'

He considered it; and then handed me back the paper.

'No. You play it.'

If I hadn't been slightly drunk, and if the place hadn't been so empty, I would never have had the nerve. Apart from anything else, I'd never even played it on a piano before, only on an electric keyboard, which isn't the same thing at all. Be that as it may, I found myself walking over to the piano, sitting down on the stool, and trying to prepare myself by breathing deeply. A couple of seconds later I had hit the first chord.

Some musicians will tell you that alcohol can improve your playing by helping you to relax. This is not true. The only real relaxation comes from feeling confident about your material. The sort of relaxation offered by alcohol is nothing but a blurring of perception, which means that faults in your performance never distract you because you don't even notice them. I was too drunk, that evening, to play a respectable version of 'Tower Hill'. Exactly how it would have sounded to an objective listener I don't know: all Tony would tell me afterwards was that I had made some mistakes. At least, that's what he told me about the first half of what I played. The rest could perhaps best be described as an excursion into free improvisation.

The fact is that after a few minutes I lost all concentration on the music and became absorbed, instead, in the associations which it brought to mind. My fingers played on, quite independent, while I thought of all those long, tired walks home from the tube station; how hopeful I'd felt, at first; how dogged and blind I had been more recently. I couldn't find it in me to be bitter, though. My mind went back more and more to those early evenings with Madeline: the fun of going to new places together and the easy flow of our conversation; the sight of her looking out for me at some meeting-point, the way her face would light up at the first glimpse of my approach. Meanwhile, on the keyboard, I must have been going through impossible key changes and dissonances, and I didn't come back to my senses until a familiar phrase struck my ear and I realized that, for some reason or other, I was playing (albeit softly and out of time) the plangent theme from 'Stranger in a Foreign Land'.

I stopped in mid-flight; and there was a deadly hush, all around me, as the customers – none of whom were talking, any more, but all looking in my direction – stared, puzzled and hostile, wondering who I was and why they were no longer listening to their regular pianist.

Hastily I got up, pushed through the tables and rejoined Tony in the corner of the room.

'I've got to go,' I said. 'I'm sorry. I must be drunk or something.'

He nodded, and looked at me with worried eyes.

'Will you be OK?' he said. 'Getting back, I mean? Do you want me to come with you?'

'I'll be OK.'

'All right then.' Just as I was leaving, he added: 'Oh, and don't forget about Sunday.'

'Sunday?'

'Not this one, the week after. You're supposed to be looking after Ben for us. Yes?'

'Oh, sure. Next Sunday. Fine.'

I staggered out, and the next thing I can remember, I was standing by the ticket barrier at Leicester Square station. I don't know whether it was by mistake or half-formed design, but instead of getting a train to Embankment, I found myself travelling north. I got out at Euston and stood on the platform long after the other passengers had left it. I needed to talk to someone. There was someone I very badly wanted to see, and this was why I had taken the northbound train. Who was it? I couldn't concentrate. What was I supposed to do next – turn around and go back home? Karla. I wanted to see Karla. What for? Was I going to tell her about this evening, about the argument, about Madeline? What time was it. Quarter past eleven. The White Goat would be closed by the time I got there. Closed, but not deserted. She would still be inside, cleaning the tables, washing the glasses, locking up. I crossed over to the City Branch platform and took a train to the Angel. I would knock on the door. She would come to the door, open it, see my face, let me in without a word. Without a word. She would be expecting me, almost. Without a word.

'Can I help you in any way, sir?'

My fist was sore and I was looking into the face of a gigantic policeman. I was standing in a back street and everything was very quiet, now that I had stopped hammering on the door of the pub.

'The pubs close at eleven o'clock, sir,' said the policeman. This was an accusation, not a helpful statement of fact, and he wielded the word 'sir' like a blunt instrument.

'I think I must have left something in there,' I stammered. 'My wallet.'

'I see, sir. Well, you'll have to wait until the morning to get it back.'

He was about forty, with a moustache, and didn't seem too threatening. I murmured something by way of thanks and started to back away. 'Have you got enough money to get home, sir?' he asked.

'Yes, it's all right. I've got a card.'

'Good night, sir.'

He watched me as I turned the corner. Five minutes later, when I came back round the corner, he was gone. The pub was dark, the door was bolted. I leant against it, my legs gave way, and I slid to the floor.

Probably I wasn't asleep for very long. I woke up shivering, but it wasn't cold that woke me. It was a sound. The street, as I have said, was quiet. I mean quiet, and not silent, because London is never silent. You don't realize this at the time, while you're living there: lying awake at four in the morning you might mistake what you are listening to for silence, but you'd be wrong. You only have to go somewhere else, out into the country, even to another town, to realize that in London there is always a hum, a rumble, a buried murmur of restless, indefinable activity. It was against this backdrop, this perpetually tense atmosphere of distant noise, that I could hear something distinct and surprising. It was a voice: a high, clear, woman's voice, singing a tune so strong and lovely that it already sounded familiar, even though I knew I had never heard it before. The voice was coming from above my head, from the sky, like an angel's.

No it wasn't. I looked up and saw, above the row of shops on the opposite side of the road, an open window. One of those shops had a sign which said 'Videos – For Sale Or For Hire'. A memory clicked into place and I rose quickly to my feet: Karla. Of course. This tune was Scottish, you could tell that just by listening to it, and the words, although I couldn't understand them, sounded as though they might have been Gaelic. Many months later, in fact, I discovered the words to this song, which is called 'The Sailor's Longing'. They included these lines:

> *Nuair chì mi eun a' falbh air sgiath,*
> *Bu mhiann leam bhith 'na chuideachd:*
> *Gu'n deanainn cùrs' air tìr mo rùin,*
> *Far bheil an sluagh ri fuireach.*

Translating them into English would give you something like this:

> When I see a bird taking to wing,
> I long to fly off with it:
> I'd set my course to the land I love,
> The land my people dwell in.

I stood and listened to her voice for I don't know how long. It seemed the most beautiful thing I had ever heard. The tune spoke of such certainty and fitness, the voice was so pure, that I forgot, in a moment, everything. I even forgot that I was drunk. It spoke to me, and what it told me was exactly what I had wanted to hear. And when it was over, leaving nothing but that strange busy stillness, I no longer wanted or needed to speak to Karla. Not then. Not now.

I had heard her sing.

Turnaround

you left your girlfriend on the platform
with this really ragged notion that you'd return
but she knows that when he goes

he really goes

MORRISSEY,
London

'I'd set my course to the land I love, The land my people
dwell in.' Well, I still wasn't ready for that: I wasn't going
to let London defeat me, yet. But my thoughts did turn
back towards home the next day, and I was reminded,
with a clarity I hadn't counted on, of some scenes from
my past life which I had been doing my best to ignore.
The reason for this was the arrival, sooner than I had
expected, of a letter from Derek.

It wasn't just a letter, in fact, but a parcel; and the first
thing I found when I opened it was a record – a seven-
inch single. The A-side was called 'Violent Life'; the B-

side was 'Insomnia'. It was credited to a band called The Dwarves of Death.

A letter was folded up inside the picture sleeve; I took it out and started reading.

Dear Bill,

Nice to hear from you – at long last. What with nobody getting a peep out of you up here, and seeing as how you haven't cropped up on Top of the Pops yet, rumours have been flying around the homestead that you must have fallen into the Thames and floated off to that great recording studio in the sky. But it turns out that you're alive and well and living in Bohemian squalor. We're all very relieved, I can tell you.

Well, you're probably wondering about the contents of this parcel. It's just another example of the astonishing efficiency of the Derek Tooley Musical Information Service Inc. All Your Pop Questions Answered. 'Name That Tune' Contestants Briefed. Fast, Reliable and Germ-Free. Your friend is absolutely right. There was indeed a band called The Dwarves of Death – one of those hundreds of forgotten little bands who sprang up during the punk era, made a couple of cheap indie singles, and disappeared without trace. Forgotten, that is, to all but a handful of memorabilia maniacs like myself. I don't have a copy of the record your friend mentioned, 'Black and Blue', but I do remember it. The one you hold in your sweaty little hand at the moment (assuming it hasn't got lost in the post, in which case the Post Office are in for a good hiding) is even rarer. It was their second (and last) single, put out on a label which even I've never come across anywhere else – probably their own. It must have been a pressing of about 100, and they may well have sold at least 6 or 7.

When you listen to this record you will find that the Dwarves tended to shun the finer feelings of the human spirit and were not given to subtlety or delicate shades of expression. 'Violent Life' offers a two-minute vision of Glasgow as urban hell: rape, mugging, gang-fights and drug abuse seem to be its main points of reference. It seems, however, like a gentle pastoral idyll beside the B-side, 'Insomnia', which, insofar as the lyrics can be made out, seems to consist of a woman screaming into the microphone at her ex-lover about how she hopes he'll never have a proper night's sleep again. It's a bit like listening to chalk being scraped across a blackboard.

Incidentally, your friend's memory is playing tricks if he thinks that the band had any bona fide dwarves in it. I can't remember the exact line-up but this seems to me highly unlikely. As for those weird hooded figures on the cover of the single, it must have been a publicity shot. They got their name (aren't you lucky to have a friend who can remember things like this?) from a newspaper headline in the Glasgow Herald which became quite a legend at the time. Apparently these two men – brothers – had just been arrested on charges of

*breaking and entering and armed robbery: they had
gone into a warehouse at night and tied up the security
guard and tried to shoot him but the gun had backfired
and wounded one of them in the arm. They were both
only about 3'6" and were known in the area for a string
of burglary offences which involved climbing through
tiny windows, but they were pretty bad at it and were
always getting caught. Vicious but incompetent, in
other words. Anyway, they were convicted on the
evidence of this security guard, and would probably
have been forgotten altogether if that sarcastic headline
hadn't stuck. Even now I can't remember their real
names or how long they were sent down for.*

*OK, that's enough pages from the scrapbook of
musical history to be going on with. Show the record
to your friend, just to settle the argument, and bring it
home with you next time you come back up to Sheffield.*

There was more to the letter but time was getting on
and I was going to be late for work. I put the single on to
my turntable, though, and turned up the volume so I
could hear it from the kitchen while I was boiling the
kettle. The record sleeve consisted of a rather grainy
photograph showing this androgynous-looking figure –
you could just about tell from her shape that it was a
woman – standing with her back to the camera looking
out over a river. Standing on either side of her, at the
water's edge, were two little people dressed in matching
cloaks, with hoods shielding their faces. The overall effect

was decidedly sinister, but the dwarves could easily have been superimposed on to the picture, I thought.

The music turned out to be a routine blast of low-grade punk, with a particularly nasty vocal over the top. That sort of thing sets my teeth on edge, I must say. The B-side was even worse, because there wasn't even any accompaniment apart from a drumbeat. I half expected Tina to come out from her room and tell me to turn it down; but, as usual, my only communication with Tina that morning was via a note:

Dear W, I may see you this evening because I feel awful and won't be going into work. Sorry about the bathroom I'll clean it up. I've pulled the plug on the answering machine if that's all right because I don't want any messages. Please be quiet in the morning. Love T.

This note, so different in tone from her usual cheerful messages, left me very unsettled. Even the handwriting seemed shaky and untidy. I read it through a couple of times but couldn't concentrate very well because of the awful screeching that was coming from my bedroom; so I ran inside and turned the record off. In the ensuing silence, I re-read the note and it seemed more disturbing than ever. Was Tina all right? Should I go into her room and see? No, surely not. Perhaps I would get a chance to find out if I spoke to her that evening: but I didn't want to stay in that evening. I wanted to meet Harry and go to The White Goat, so I could show him the record, and (of course) see Karla. Should I put this visit off, and stay in with Tina instead?

I decided against it and set off for work, taking the single with me in a plastic carrier-bag. As an afterthought, I plugged the answering machine in again. I wasn't going to let Tina's whims spoil my chances of getting a job.

*

At lunchtime I phoned Harry and arranged to meet him for a drink that evening; and I read the rest of Derek's letter.

> Nothing much has happened up here that will appear exciting to a big-city dweller like yourself. I'm still working down at Harper's and there's talk of me becoming deputy shop-steward next year. The job is fairly safe but you have to keep your ear to the ground round here as you never know who is going to get the chop next. Meanwhile I'm always on the look-out for jobs with bigger firms, and I even had an interview in Manchester a couple of months ago, but it didn't come to anything. Too many people chasing too few jobs, as usual.
>
> The music business seems to be in as shocking a state as ever, with accountants and stock-brokers holding sway and post-modernist pirates rifling through old record collections looking for anything half-way decent from the sixties that can be plundered and decked out

*in 1980s fashions. I trust this will all be put to rights
when the biscuit factory or whatever you're called gets
its act together and takes the charts by storm. My only
advice is this: for God's sake find yourselves a good
hairdresser.*

*That's it for now and I hope maybe to hear from you
sometime in the next ten years. Keep on rocking, and
all that, and look after yourself.*

    Regards,

     Derek.

*P.S. I've seen Stacey a few times recently and she's
looking happy and as well as ever. In fact I saw her
last night and told her I'd had your letter and asked if
there was any message. She said, 'Don't forget the
phone, Bill.' – D.*

I smiled at this message, which I recognized as being
at once a rebuke and a coded intimacy. It was one of those
not particularly witty or original jokes which you will
always find in the private language of lovers. I couldn't
even remember when we first started using it. It must
have been after I had become a student, I suppose: when
I was at Leeds.

The funny thing about me and Stacey, it seems to me
now, is that we never really split up. We broke off the
engagement, yes, but we didn't actually stop seeing each
other. My memory of the order in which things happened
starts to get very confused here. Feelings ran deep

between Stacey and me but they were never overt. Decisions were taken, often quite major decisions, without either of us realizing it, sometimes, and certainly without a lot of discussion or heart-searching. I can remember telling her that I had decided to leave Boots and go to university in Leeds, and she accepted the idea without a murmur of disagreement. I suppose it wasn't as if I was going to be far away. Perhaps that was the first time, round about then, that she said, 'Don't forget the phone, Bill.'

If I were to call Stacey down to earth, it wouldn't be because she was unglamorous. On the contrary, with her cropped but slightly curly black hair, her wide shoulders and slender hips, she was always attracting attention from men. And if I were to call her uncomplaining, I wouldn't want it to sound as though she was weak, or had no mind of her own. Maybe a better word would be 'unflappable'. A slightly worrying theory occurs to me, which is that she saw right into the heart of me from day one, knew me through and through, knew exactly what to expect from me and so was never surprised when I behaved badly or put a difficult decision before her. In all my floundering, all my efforts to carve out a life for myself up there, she was always one step ahead of me. I dare say she'd already worked out for herself that it would be a good idea if I went to university, and was just waiting for me to realize it too.

We were engaged by then, but perhaps even so she saw it as the beginning of the end of our relationship, and accepted the fact, as readily as she accepted the prospect of my frequent absences. We continued to see each other, most weekends – sometimes in Leeds but more usually in Sheffield, where we would stay either with her family or mine, taking pleasure in being under the same roof even though provincial proprieties would not allow us to share a bed. Every Sunday, if it was a reasonable day, we would go walking up on the dales. Our favourite was to take a bus out to The Fox House, and then walk down the valley to Grindleford railway station, just by the Totley tunnel. It was a walk which could change dramatically with every season, and we did it in deep snow and bright sunshine; the leaves brilliant with the colours of spring or turning to copper against blue, autumnal skies.

That was how things were for the first couple of terms, anyway. When did it start to go wrong? When did we realize – long after the event, presumably – that we had become no more than a habit to one another, that the freshness and the admiration which we had taken for granted had faded into mere tolerance? To a sort of lazy familiarity, in fact, which was worse than indifference. I can't even remember which of us suggested breaking off the engagement; what I can remember (and it seems peculiar, at this distance) is that we were more affectionate towards each other, that evening, than we had been for months. After that, there was a gradual drifting apart. Maybe she was seeing somebody else, or maybe she thought I was. I went back to Leeds to start my second year, continued to write to her occasionally, even saw her once or twice at weekends. We weren't in each other's thoughts much, for a while.

The last time I really spoke to her was the weekend I came down to Sheffield to say goodbye to my parents. We went on the same walk again, even though it was a grey and misty morning, and as we sat beside the edge of the stream, eating the sandwiches which Stacey's mother had made for us, I told her:

'I've decided to give up my degree.'

'I know,' she said.

'Who told you?'

'Derek. You're going to go down to London, and become a musician.'

'Are you surprised?'

'No. I thought you might.'

I turned to her and said, earnestly, as she munched an egg mayonnaise sandwich, 'I just think that if I don't try now, I may be leaving it too late. I mean, chemistry's something I can always come back to, and – '

She interrupted me.

'You don't have to justify yourself to me, Bill. I know the kind of person you are. I think it's good.'

I smiled, thankful, and didn't try to explain further.

'Have you got somewhere to stay?'

'Tony – my piano teacher – he's down there now. His sister-in-law's got a flat and that'll do to be going on with.'

'When are you going?'

'Soon. Next week some time.'

Stacey said, 'Let me know when. Will you, please? Will you be going from here?'

'Yes.'

'I'll take some time off work. I'll come and see you off at the station.'

'Don't be silly, you don't have to do that.'

'I want to, though. I think it's important.'

And so she was there at the station that morning, along with my mother. We didn't get a chance to talk properly – you never do, on these occasions – and I can't remember much that we said; but I'd be surprised if she didn't find time to take me aside at some point and say – smiling, of course – 'Don't forget the phone, Bill.'

I hadn't contacted her once since coming down to London.

*

Stacey had been eclipsed by Madeline; and that seems strange, in a way. Stranger still, though, is the thought that, temporarily at least, both of them had been eclipsed by Karla, and by that single, crystalline image I had of her voice cutting through the half-silence of a London night. I could hardly wait to get up to The White Goat that evening to tell her about it. I stopped off at a hamburger place on the way, bolted down some food, and arrived at the pub shortly after six o'clock.

Unfortunately I had forgotten how crowded it would be, this being Friday evening. She was being kept busy behind the bar, with a whole row of men's faces lined up in front of her, waving money and barking orders, and although she nodded a friendly 'Hello' to me as I asked for my first drink, it wasn't until I came back for my second that we managed to get talking. Even then, there was a crowd of people around, and I only had half her attention.

'Can we talk?' I said in a loud whisper.

'Sure,' she answered.

'I mean – there's something I want to tell you.'

'Can't it wait?'

'Well . . . maybe when things have quietened down a bit.'

She shook her head.

'Fridays are like this all night. What's the matter, is it something personal?'

'Well yes, in a manner of – '

Just then some bloke in a suit with a wad of ten-pound notes in his hand cut across me and started ordering about fifteen lagers. While Karla was pulling them, I followed her up the bar and said:

'It's about something that happened last night.'

'Oh yes?'

I paused, and announced, in a low voice: 'I heard you.'

'What do you mean?' she said, not looking up from her work.

'I mean I was there. Outside your window, last night.'

She stared at me.

'What are you talking about?'

'It was absolutely beautiful. I've never heard anything like it.'

'A few packets of dry roasted, too, while you're at it, love,' the customer shouted. 'And a box of Hamlets.'

'Are you some kind of pervert or something?' she said.

'Don't be silly. I wasn't following you, or anything like that. It's just that I wanted a word with you last night, but after I'd heard you singing I didn't have to. I just listened and then went away again.'

'Listen.' She left the pumps and faced me squarely across the bar. 'For your information – and not that it's any of your business – I didn't get back till two in the morning last night. I was round at a friend's place. So I don't know what the *hell* you're talking about.' She turned to her customer. 'How many packets was it?'

'Four'll do. Thanks.'

'I mean – you don't even know where I live.'

'Yes I do. You told me you lived right opposite here, above the video shop.'

She went to fetch the peanuts, and when she came back I continued: 'I stood outside your window – it was open – and there was this woman singing. She was Scottish, she was singing a Scottish song.' I voiced the awful question: 'It was you, wasn't it?'

The customer paid her, she took the money and before going over to the till she said, impatiently: 'That's the flat below mine. There are a couple of hippies in there. They're always getting pissed and playing their bloody folk records at top volume. The whole building stinks of real ale and roll-ups. You've only given me twelve, here,' she added, to the man in the suit.

'Sorry.'

He gave her the extra money and I stood there, feeling more stupid than I'd felt in a long while.

'Do you have to stand at the bar?' she said. 'It makes it hard to serve the other customers.'

There was a small table free in the corner, so I went and sat down. If I hadn't arranged to meet Harry, I would have run out of the pub there and then. But it wasn't just that I had made a fool of myself in front of Karla: that was bad enough, but what really shocked me was the light it threw on my behaviour yesterday. Was my commitment to Madeline really that feeble? Was I really so lazy about putting any work into that relationship? We had had one little argument – our first genuine argument for months – and instead of following her and attempting to resolve the issue I had gone off on my own, full of self-pity, got drunk, behaved like an idiot in Samson's, and then gone to eavesdrop outside the flat of another woman, someone I had barely met but for whom I had felt, the last time I saw her, a vague physical attraction. It was pathetic. No wonder Madeline had been angry with me. Somehow or other, I was going to have to get back in touch with her and make a big effort: some gesture – a present, perhaps – flamboyant but sincere, which would convince Madeline once and for all that I was in earnest about her.

I put this proposition to Harry, after he had arrived and I had shown him the record (which gave him considerable satisfaction).

'What was this argument about, exactly?' he asked. He seemed a bit nervous talking about it, because affairs of the heart weren't his strong point, and besides (as I think I mentioned) I had never spoken to him about Madeline before.

'Well, I don't really know. That's the problem. She was late arriving, and we quarrelled about that a bit. Then things got even worse and I asked her if something was the matter and she said she wanted . . . a change.'

'What sort of change?'

'A change in the relationship.'

Harry frowned.

'What sort of change in the relationship?'

'I don't know, do I? If I knew that, then I wouldn't be asking you about it.'

I sipped my Becks angrily while Harry sat there looking sheepish. Finally he said: 'Perhaps she wants you to get married.'

I looked at him in astonishment.

'What?'

'Perhaps that's what she meant, when she said she wanted a change. Perhaps she meant . . . marriage.'

I considered this for a moment.

'Are you serious?'

'It's just a thought. I don't know much about these things.'

After a pause, I said, 'She would have said so, wouldn't she, if that's what she meant?'

Harry shrugged. 'I don't know. Women are funny about things like that.'

I shook my head. 'No, it's ridiculous. She must have meant something else.'

'Like what?'

'Well . . .' No alternative suggested itself to me. 'But that's crazy – I mean, I'm not in a position to marry her.'

'True. But that's not to stop you *asking*. She might just want that feeling of, you know, security.'

I was still trying to come to terms with this suggestion when I heard Karla's peremptory voice behind me.

'Excuse me, would you?'

She wanted to wipe our table down, and the record was in the way. I removed it, she gave the table a quick, careless wipe with a damp cloth, and left without saying anything else. A distinct chill remained after she'd gone.

'I thought you were quite friendly with her,' said Harry.

'Oh, she's just busy tonight, that's all.'

I lapsed into silence again, and when Harry next spoke, his tone was gloomy.

'I've been listening to the tape we made on Tuesday.'

'And?'

He shook his head meaningfully.

'As bad as that?'

'I think we'd be wasting time and money if we tried to send it off to anybody.'

I sighed. 'I knew we should have done a different song.'

I was just fishing for a compliment here, and he duly took the bait.

'It's not the song. It's a great song. But the whole thing doesn't gel: it sounds a mess. Perhaps we didn't have enough time to rehearse it.' Looking forlornly into the middle distance, he said, 'Shit. I really did want this one to work, too.' He drained off the last of his beer. 'We're in a mess, Bill, we really are.'

*

I was in a mess, too. For the second night in a row, I was drunk. Even though Harry had been with me this time, it was a joyless experience. When I got back to the flat, shortly after midnight, I could hardly fit my key into the lock, and I was conscious of making an enormous amount of noise as I clattered around and started to run the bath. There was no sound from Tina's room, and her door was firmly closed. Perhaps she'd gone to work after all. I pushed the door open and looked in: after a few seconds, I could make out her sleeping body. She was breathing deeply and lying on her side. Everything seemed all right.

They're good things, baths. You can get a lot done in a bath, in my experience. Thinking, I mean. It was while I was in the bath that night that I had my brainwave, and the two problems I had been discussing with Harry – the problem with Madeline, and the problem with our tape – suddenly cohered: it seemed a sort of natural miracle, as when two elements react together to form a completely new compound.

It wasn't by means of a conscious thought-process, either. I was singing the tune to myself in the bath, the tune of 'Stranger in a Foreign Land': only where I should have been singing the words 'Now and then', at the beginning of the verse, I was singing 'Madeline' instead. It seemed to fit perfectly. And all at once I thought – well, it would only take a few more changes, and the whole song could be about her. Better still, it could be *for* her. And what about that line – 'When I'm down, will you carry me?' There was something else, surely, that was crying out to be sung there: 'Madeline – will you marry me?'

A marriage proposal in the form of a song. Words and music entirely by myself. If Harry was right, and this was what Madeline had really been trying to tell me that evening, how could she possibly resist such a novel approach? What better way, not only to bring about a reconciliation, but to put everything on an entirely new footing? It had been music which had brought us together in the first place, so it was only right that it should be music – my music – which should heal this temporary rift and ensure that nothing like it would ever happen again.

Five minutes later, still wet from the bath, I was telephoning Harry.

'Bill, it's nearly one o'clock,' he said, in a voice heavy with sleep. 'This had better be important.'

'I've been thinking,' I said. 'It's not too late to do something about that song. I'm going to write some new words and we can record the whole thing again.' There was silence from his end. 'Well?'

'I can't see Martin and Jake jumping at that idea, to be honest.'

'Never mind about them, we could do it ourselves – just you and me. Look, I can come over tomorrow and we can write a drum pattern together on your machine. Then we can take it into the studio on Sunday and get it all done in less than four hours. I'm sure of it.'

'What about the guitar part?'

'You can do that. Let's face it, Harry, you're better than Martin anyway.'

He went silent again, and I could tell that he was coming round to the idea.

'New words, you say?'

'Yes. New words. Don't worry about those. Leave those to me.'

★

It was now early December, 1988: a time of bleak and perfunctory afternoons and long dark evenings. Winter is a bad time to be in London, even a mild winter like this one. Some people manage to make themselves comfortable: I could imagine, for instance, that for Mrs Gordon, tucked up between linen sheets in her Kensington mansion, with Madeline always on call to bring her tea and buttered toast at the touch of a bell, the passing of the seasons might have made very little difference. It was easy to forget, at times, that such people existed and that such lives were lived. I had little to complain about, myself. I had a roof over my head and a cheap one at that; a couple of miles away, men and women were sleeping in cardboard boxes under Waterloo bridge. So it wasn't a sense of material hardship which made me shiver and ache for better things, as I battled against the wind on my way to the studio through the grounds of Guy's Hospital (the coldest and windiest place in London). It was four o'clock on a Sunday afternoon, the world was getting dark, and I tried to promise myself that there would not be many more afternoons like this, afternoons when I would stagger along with my keyboard under my arm from one hopeless engagement to another, the ambition which was meant to be driving me on nothing but a memory, lodged in my brain like a dead weight. All that would change. Not that I thought the tape we were about to make would ever impress a record company (even if it got as far as one): I had more or less given up on The Alaska Factory. But I was confident of the impression it would make on Madeline; and confident, too, that if I had before me the prospect of marrying her, I would feel a new sense of responsibility which might force me to think harder and more intelligently about my career.

Funnily enough, I look back on that recording session with some fondness. The fact that Jake and Martin weren't there, and knew nothing about it, put us in a conspiratorial mood and infected the whole occasion with a sort of cheerfulness which I didn't normally associate with Thorn Bird Studios. The only real argument we had was at the very beginning, over the changes I had made to the lyrics. At first Harry couldn't believe I was being serious, but I pointed out to him that it was his idea that I should propose to Madeline, originally, and besides, he had to admit that in this version the song was definitely more memorable.

For instance, the second half now went like this:

> Madeline
> You look at me without a murmur
> The time has come
> To make the bond between us firmer
>
> I'll give you every token
> Precious gifts from out of Araby
> Why am I heartbroken?
> Oh Madeline, will you marry me?

Harry shook his head.

'I can't sing this,' he kept saying. 'I don't even know the woman.'

All the same, I soon talked him round to it.

As usual we got precious little joy out of Vincent. I suppose it was our fault for antagonizing him to start with. I hadn't been able to resist bringing the Dwarves of

Death record along with me, just to prove that he had been wrong. His initial reaction had been one of surly disbelief; he took the record off me and said that he wanted to look at it more closely. I hate people who can't bear to lose an argument. After that he didn't talk to us much, just sat in the control booth reading a back issue of *Midi Mania* while making occasional adjustments to the faders. At the end, when we asked him how it had sounded, he said: 'Brilliant. I should get on the phone to EMI right away, if I was you. Which one of you's going to have the golden disc on his bedroom wall, then? Or do you both share the same bedroom, eh? Har, har, har!'

Then a strange thing happened: when we asked him to give us the record back, he couldn't find it. He claimed to have taken it upstairs with him and left it on his desk, and now it had disappeared.

'Typical!' he said. 'I should know better than to leave anything lying around in this place. The kind of low-life I get in here, they're no better than criminals, most of them.'

'Look, that wasn't even my record,' I said. 'It belonged to a friend of mine. And it's extremely rare.'

I was appalled to think what Derek might say when I told him that I'd lost it. Nevertheless, Vincent was blithely unapologetic, and to make things even worse he charged us twice as much for the session as we had been expecting.

'Your manager didn't tell me anything about this,' he said, 'so I'm going to have to charge you normal rates.'

'The man's a total bastard,' said Harry, as we sat, a few minutes later, in a café near London Bridge station, eating sausage and chips. 'I reckon he stole that record himself. He probably knows how much it's worth on the collectors' market.'

I nodded, and chased a recalcitrant baked bean around my plate before saying, 'It makes you wonder about Chester a bit, doesn't it?'

'What do you mean?'

'Well, how come Chester manages to get on with him? How do you come to have such a good business arrangement with a man like that?'

'That's the sign of a good manager, though, isn't it? Being able to get on the right side of different sorts of people.'

I considered this and shook my head.

'No, there's more to it than that.' I tapped my fork against the table in frustration. 'There's something going *on* at that place, and I don't know what it is. You know Karla, the woman behind the bar at The White Goat?'

'Yes?'

'She doesn't trust Chester. She says she sees him there all the time, with all sorts of strange people. And last Sunday, just after we'd all had that . . . discussion, this bloke came in. Paisley, his name was – he's the lead singer with this other band that Chester manages. And he was desperate for a fix or something. In the end they went off together.'

'You think Chester was supplying him?'

'Maybe. And if Chester's involved in all that scene, what about Vincent? Where does he come in?'

'Don't get carried away, Bill. Vincent's just a mean-minded little bastard, that's all. I don't think he's up to anything shady.'

'So what does he keep in Studio B? You're not telling me that's *really* a rehearsal room. Nobody's allowed to go near the place.'

Harry resumed his eating. 'Sorry,' he said. 'You've lost me.'

I leant forward, and said in an urgent whisper: 'I heard *voices* behind that door, Harry. I'm sure of it.'

'If you ask me, you're letting your imagination get the better of you. In any case it's none of your business, and the less I know about what that guy gets up to in his spare time, the happier I'll be. At the moment, I'm more interested in *this*.'

From his coat pocket, he brought out the spool of tape containing the new version of 'Madeline (Stranger in a Foreign Land)'.

I smiled.

'How do you think it went?'

'Pretty good. Pretty bloody good. Probably the best thing we've done.'

I thought so too, but it was reassuring to have it confirmed. Using the drum machine had enabled us to create, at last, exactly the rhythm we wanted, with some extra effects like shakers and handclaps, and Harry had added a funky little guitar pattern which went against the basic drumbeat: it gave the whole song a far busier and more purposeful feel. The new words I had written were easier to sing, and he had slightly altered the vocal part anyway to bring it within his range. It was an enormous improvement on our other effort.

'I'll buy some tapes tomorrow and get about a dozen copies done,' he said. 'I've already been to see a printer about the inlay cards. He said I could pick them up tomorrow.'

'What did you put on them?'

'I just said who was in the band, and I credited Vincent as producer, and I gave a phone number.'

'Whose phone number?'

'Yours. You're the one with the answering machine.'

'Fair enough. I'd like a couple of copies as soon as possible, then.'

'A couple?'

'Well, one for me, and one . . .'

'Yes?'

I didn't bother to spell it out, and Harry was too nice to want to tease me about it. All he said, with a friendly smile, was 'Good luck.'

*

It was not quite midnight, this time, when I got back to the flat, and Tina was awake for once. There was a light coming from the kitchen, where she was sitting at the table with her back to the door.

'Hello,' I said, agreeably surprised.

She answered, 'Hello, William,' without looking

round. 'I was just going to write you a note, only now I needn't bother.'

'Oh. Anything important?'

'Only to say that you still owe me for rent, and that I'd drunk some of your milk. You don't mind, do you?'

'No, not at all.'

It was the first time we had spoken for weeks. It seemed absurd that we should have so little to say to each other.

'Is Pedro coming round tonight?' I asked.

'He's already been.'

'Oh.'

Tina got up, and with a slow, careful movement she pulled her green cotton dressing-gown tightly around her.

'I'm going to bed.'

She walked quickly past me, and neither of us said good night. Her face was badly bruised, her throat red with finger marks.

Key Change

So, goodbye
please stay with your own kind
and I'll stay with mine

MORRISSEY,
Miserable Lie

Anyway, back to that night. The night of the murder, I mean. I've been doing my best to put it off, but there's nothing more to tell you, now, apart from how it ended. I don't relish the prospect, to be honest. Recently I've been trying to forget these events – not so much because of the details, which are a bit unpleasant, I admit, but because it frightens me to recall the state I was in. Psychologically. I hope to God that nothing like that ever happens to me again. I'll try not to exaggerate, and I'll try to say exactly what I mean: and for your part, you must take these words and really think about them. Because that night, I felt – and it's the most terrible feeling, the worst feeling I know – that an entire world was slipping out of my grasp.

The thing that really surprised me, the one thing I had never expected about terror (never having experienced it before) was how bloody *sad* it made me feel. I sat there on that bus and I swear to you it was all I could do to keep myself from crying. It seemed that I was saying goodbye to so much, you see. Everything I had been working towards for the last few years had turned to nonsense. Not just all the music; not just all the effort I had put into living in London. Even the simple peace of mind enjoyed by the other passengers on the bus that evening – that was denied me now, as well. The only assumption I had ever made about my life – that it would never lose sight of a basic sanity and normality – had been casually shot to pieces.

Even as I realized this, more and more details of the murder were coming back to me. It was a strange, but undeniable, fact that the picture on the record sleeve Derek had sent me – the attitude adopted by the two dwarves, standing apart and looking straight ahead, face-less, impassive – was uncannily reminiscent of Paisley's assassins. But as soon as I tried to get any further, to imagine how there could possibly be a means of piecing together these clues, my head began to spin, and there seemed to be no point of entry. It defied logic.

There was nothing to be gained from trying to sort it out anyway. It wasn't my job to find out what was at the bottom of this crazy business – who was trying to kill who, and why, and what particular manner of illegal activity they were all engaged in at the time. I was only a musician, after all. I dealt in first inversions and augmented fourths, not crack or heroin, and I'd never even had a parking ticket before now or been caught watching the television without a licence. And now my reward, apparently, for twenty-three scrupulous years of law-abiding citizenship, was to have my life wrecked at a stroke by the stupid antics of a bunch of people I'd hardly met and had no connection with.

I closed my eyes and tried to pretend that it wasn't happening. For a while my mind went blank; and when I did start thinking again, some minutes later, it was along quite different lines.

Back at the beginning of this story, I remember mentioning something which had caught my eye as Chester drove me through Islington. From the front seat of his car, my gaze had been drawn to the lit windows of Georgian terraced houses: kitchens and dining-rooms golden with lamplight as families prepared their evening meals and poured themselves pre-dinner drinks. If I had felt excluded from these scenes at the time, I felt infinitely more so now – but all the same, as I remembered them, and as the bus continued to carry me on in God knows what direction, a fantasy arose within me. Why shouldn't I be allowed to live like that? Why should I let these senseless, random circumstances defeat me? I had a girlfriend. She lived in a beautiful house. There was no reason, no reason on earth, why I shouldn't spend this evening with her.

For the first time, I looked out of the window of the bus, and instantly recognized the area: we were heading towards Kensington.

So Madeline had made no attempt to contact me since I sent her the tape; but what could be more natural? She would have been astonished, stunned, thoroughly taken aback by the realization that my intentions were far more serious than she had imagined. It was even possible that she didn't know whether to accept or not. What she needed, in all probability, was the chance to talk it over with me, face to face.

Suppose I were to turn up there, now, with a bottle of champagne? A bottle of champagne, and a bunch of flowers? A bottle of champagne, a bunch of flowers, and a box of assorted continental chocolates? Apart from anything else, it would be safer than going back to my own flat, because nobody knew of my association with Madeline (apart from Tony and Harry, and even they had no idea where she lived). I could stay there for days, and nobody would ever find me. I could turn up, laden with gifts, I could tell her what had happened, she would comfort me, and then we could have a long and earnest talk about our relationship. We'd pop out to the all-night grocer's, buy in some tagliatelle or rigatoni or something, cook a meal together, and then settle down with a couple of glasses of red wine and make some serious plans for our future. Finally, at around midnight, it would be time for bed. We would steal shy looks at the corner of the room, make embarrassing remarks about fetching a spare mattress and some blankets, but neither of us would mean it. I would still be in a state of shock, I would shrink from the idea of sleeping alone, and Madeline would sense this, instinctively. She would draw me gently towards the bed. I would sit there, she would stand before me and lay her hands on my shoulders and fix me with her grave grey eyes. Then, turning off all but the bedside light . . .

Where the fuck could I get a box of continental chocolates at this time of night?

For the next few minutes, at any rate, things went in my favour. I got off the bus at South Kensington and found an off-licence which also sold chocolates. Not far along the road, a florist was just putting the shutters down on his shop. I persuaded him to let me in and for three pounds fifty I was given a little bunch of manky carnations. Even though it wasn't particularly late in the evening, I now felt as though I was in a frantic hurry, and I ran all the way to Mrs Gordon's house. Before ringing the bell, I had to lean for a while against those massive oak doors in order to get my breath back.

Here, away from the West End, away from the traffic, away from just about any sign of humanity apart from the occasional pedestrian, it seemed incredibly quiet. A thin, frozen mist was hanging in the air; it mingled with my breath whenever I exhaled. Visibility was poor. If someone were to approach, discreet footsteps against the pavement would announce their imminence long before they actually emerged from the gloom. I could barely make out the tall hedge on the other side of the street.

Mrs Gordon's house was in darkness, utter darkness. I could see at once that Madeline wasn't in, but I rang the bell anyway. As you may have noticed, my mind wasn't working very sensibly that evening. At first there was no answer and I thought that there must be nobody in the house at all. I rang the bell again, twice. Nothing. What about the cook? Wouldn't she be there? Surely the whole household couldn't have packed up and gone away, without Madeline even telling me about it. I rang the bell again, long and insistently.

There is nothing like a single, loud noise, for making the surrounding quiet seem even more absolute. When you are in the country, and a dog barks in the middle of the night, it merely punctuates and emphasizes the silence, making you hear it all the more keenly. Similarly, when I stopped ringing the bell, there descended a hush so sudden, and so still, that it seemed as if the mist had managed to cushion even London's usual ceaseless hum. I stood waiting, feeling despair begin to creep into my bones, like the cold. I shivered and hugged the plastic carrier-bag containing my gifts. Now and again I stood back from the house and looked up at its dark, curtained windows.

Then, all at once, a light came on. It was on the first floor. A few moments later I could see a shadow moving behind a curtain. I went to the doorbell and rang again, pressing it four or five times. It was all I could do to stop myself from shouting out.

Nothing further happened for some time. Eventually, after I had rung the bell another half-dozen times, and run back and forth, up and down the steps which led to the doorway, trying to get a glimpse of what was going on upstairs, another light came on: this time it was the light in the hall, shining out through a glass panel above the front door. By climbing up on to the railings, I could just about raise myself to the level of this panel and see through it. I could see a tiny, fragile old woman coming slowly down the huge stairway, supporting herself awkwardly on a wooden stick. She was wearing a thick, pale blue dressing-gown. I jumped back down at once in case she saw me and took fright at the sight of my wild, staring eyes. Stupidly I tried to straighten my coat and brush back my hair, making tiny last-minute adjustments to my appearance. Nothing could have stopped me from looking like an escaped madman.

On the other side of the door, I could hear her slippered feet shuffling across the floor, and the soft thud of her walking stick against the marble. I could tell that she was only a few inches away. Now the letterbox was pushed open and a thin voice emerged:

'Who is it? What do you want?'

Trying to make myself sound civilized and reassuring, I bent down to the letterbox and said: 'My name's William. I want to speak to Madeline.'

When she answered, I could see her puckered old lips mouthing the words.

'Madeline's not here. You'll have to go away.'

'I'm a friend of hers. A very good friend. I've been here before, lots of times. I must see Madeline tonight.'

There was a short silence, during which I thought that she had turned around and was going back upstairs; but then I heard bolts being pulled back and the turning of a key. The door swung open and Mrs Gordon was standing before me. She was a very small woman: she had to look up to study my face.

'Why?' she said.

Explaining, obviously, was impossible.

'It's personal.'

'Madeline's a very nice girl,' said Mrs Gordon, opening the door further and letting me in. 'I like her very much. You say you're a friend of hers. I hope you haven't got her into any trouble.'

She eyed me with suspicion. I could hardly blame her.

'No,' I said. 'It's nothing like that at all.'

'She's gone out for the evening,' she said. 'You can't wait for her, because she probably won't be back until late.' Then she asked: 'You did say you were a *close* friend of Madeline's?'

'Yes.'

'Do you know what day it is?'

So the old bat was senile, it seemed. Still, I could see no harm in humouring her.

'It's Saturday,' I said.

She looked at me with a very penetrating gaze.

'Look – ' She was making me uncomfortable, and I was anxious to leave. 'I really don't want to disturb you any more. Do you know where she's gone?'

'She's round at her friend's house.'

'Her friend?'

'You know, her friend. Piers.'

'*Piers?*'

I practically shouted the name. As soon as I heard it, a sort of madness seized me, as any number of suppressed fears and hunches began to emerge from the shadows at the corners of my mind, where they had been lurking for months.

'Where does he live?'

'I've no idea.'

'The *bastard*!'

Mrs Gordon raised her stick and prodded me in the stomach with it.

'You'll be careful not to use language like that, in this house.'

'If that bastard . . . If she and that *fucking* bastard – '

'I think you'd better leave. Now.'

'I know – her address book!'

I dodged round Mrs Gordon and made for the staircase.

'Don't you dare go up there!' she shouted. 'I'll call the police.'

But I was already on my way up, and within a few seconds I was in Madeline's room. It took me no time at all to find her address book, which she kept beside the telephone. I also guessed that she would be the kind of person who listed her friends by Christian name rather than surname. Sure enough, there was Piers, under P. I memorized the address and was about to close the book when for some reason I couldn't resist looking to see if my own name was there: I turned to W.

Madeline had beautiful handwriting, there was no denying it. She had written my name in capitals, in red felt pen, and beneath it was the address of Tina's flat and my phone number. Tears sprang to my eyes as I stared at it. And then I looked around her room, her room which was so familiar to me and which seemed so strange this evening because Madeline herself wasn't there, and because everything, suddenly, had changed. The murder I had witnessed in Islington seemed insignificant now beside the suspicions which had started to crowd in on me, and it rapidly became too painful to sit there, assaulted by memories, fighting them off. I swore, got to my feet, and ran back downstairs.

Mrs Gordon was standing by the telephone in the hallway, with her back to the wall.

'I called the police,' she said. 'They're coming round.'

I said nothing and walked straight past her. I slammed the door behind me, then set off through the cold London night in the direction of Piers' apartment. I still had my carrier-bag full of chocolates, flowers and champagne.

It wasn't until much later that evening that I realized the stupidity of what I had done: I could scarcely, in fact, have devised a better way of incriminating myself further than by bursting into an old lady's house, and frightening her to the point where she would call the police and issue them (presumably) with a description which tallied exactly with the one they had already received. Like a fish caught in a net, I had writhed and struggled and achieved nothing except to get into an even worse tangle than before. All I can say, once again, is – believe me: you don't think of these things at the time.

I don't know that I was thinking at all, as I strode along through the wealthy, imperturbable streets of South Kensington, across the Fulham Road and on through Chelsea towards World's End. Once I was in the general area I had to ask for directions: but it didn't take long for me to find the address. I found myself standing outside a tall, narrow terrace; it was in darkness except for the second floor, which was brightly lit and full of the noise of voices and loud disco music. A party seemed to be in progress.

Immediately, my spirits rose. If Piers was giving a party, then of course he would invite Madeline; and if she wasn't seeing me that evening, then of course she would go. Perhaps I had jumped to entirely the wrong conclusion. Perhaps my vision of an evening alone with Madeline was still within my grasp, after all.

I rang the bell and before long a young, well-dressed young woman had come to let me in.

'I'm a friend of Madeline's,' I said. 'I've come to the party.'

'Sure.'

She gave me an odd look, which I put down to my appearance. My raincoat was dirty and crumpled at the best of times, and now, with my plastic carrier-bag and my tousled hair, I must have cut a peculiar figure. I followed her up two flights of stairs and was left standing in the hallway of a small, crowded flat while she went to find Madeline.

'Chuck your coat in one of the bedrooms,' she said, 'and put the booze in the fridge. I'll just go and get her.'

I stayed where I was. None of the other guests tried to introduce themselves to me. They all seemed to be called things like Jocasta and Jeremy, and were all wearing outfits which must have cost more money than I would have thought of spending on a year's wardrobe. They gave me a wide berth, and sneaked glances at me with wary, amused eyes which made my cheeks burn.

Shortly afterwards, Madeline emerged from one of the other rooms. She looked absolutely wonderful. She was wearing a navy blue velvet party dress with a low V-neck at the front and back, with a string of tiny pearls around her throat. She looked pale, healthy and happy. As soon as she saw me, her face fell.

'William?' she said. 'What on earth are you doing here?'

I rushed towards her, put the bag down and tried to hug her.

'Oh Madeline, you wouldn't believe what I've been through today. I've got to – '

She pushed me away.

'For God's sake, William, what are you doing? Not here.'

We stood apart. She stared at me accusingly.

'I brought you these,' I said.

From the bag I brought out the box of chocolates, which was squashed, and the flowers, which were crushed. Two of the carnations' heads had come off completely. She smiled when she saw the gift but it was a pitying smile, one I could have done without.

'How did you know?' she asked.

'Know what?'

Her smile broadened.

'That it was my birthday, of course.'

I gripped the box of chocolates tightly and tried to say something, but at first the words wouldn't come. My mind went back to Mrs Gordon's inexplicable question – 'Do you know what day it is?'

'This is . . . *your* birthday party?'

'Of course it is. Piers very kindly said I could give a party in his flat. How did you get the address?'

Before I had time to answer, Piers himself appeared. He slid his arm around Madeline's waist and said, 'Darling, Charles is just putting that new tape on. Do I know your friend?'

Our eyes met and mine were the first to look away. Madeline turned towards him, put her hand on his shoulder and said, 'No, this isn't a good time to play it now. Take it off – please? Quickly.'

But it was too late. From the next room I could hear the familiar opening of 'Stranger in a Foreign Land': high, bright chords on the keyboard, shakers setting the tempo and the mood, and that strong, plangent figure from the sampled saxophone.

'Why not?' Piers was saying. 'I think it's smashing.'

I pushed past him and stood in the doorway of the room, watching the other guests as they danced to my music. In spite of myself I couldn't help feeling a certain grim satisfaction when I saw how well 'Stranger in a Foreign Land' was working as a party record. If the other members of The Alaska Factory had been there, I would have turned to them and said, 'I told you so'. But it would have seemed like an old triumph, now. I had already moved on.

Madeline touched my arm and said, 'William, can we go and talk? Let's go into one of the bedrooms for a minute.'

I looked past her, only half-listening. That key change from D major to F: that was really neat. I couldn't have written something like that a year or two ago.

'Look – I thought you knew what I was saying that night. When I said I wanted a change. And then I didn't hear from you, so I thought ... well, that you'd understood.'

'But I sent you this song.'

'Yes I know, but – you must have written it ages ago, didn't you?'

'No, I wrote it last week.'

She followed me as I made for the door.

'Does Piers know that I wrote it?' I asked. 'Has he listened to the words?'

She shook her head.

'I don't think so. He's not very interested in music.'

A riposte occurred to me at this point: something about them being suited to each other, in that case. But I didn't say it. There's a time and a place for everything, if you ask me.

*

Sometimes, all you can do is try and wipe things from your memory. As far as the rest of that night is concerned, I've done a pretty good job, and there's nothing much to tell. One thing I do remember is the cold. I've never known cold like it. I suppose I could have gone inside somewhere, an all-night café or something, or a hotel, but I was too frightened, you see. Frightened of being seen. I went to a park. Several parks, in all probability, although they start to blur in my mind. I can remember going further into the centre of town, early in the morning it must have been, avoiding the queues for the night buses, ignoring the taxi touts and the beggars who kept coming up and asking me (me!) for money. I can remember heading down towards the river, sitting on some steps for a while. Steps that led into the water. I can't find words to describe the cold. It was there – yes, it was there – that it started to get light. I watched the sickly dawn spreading itself over the Thames. I drank a whole bottle of champagne and ate a whole box of assorted continental chocolates. I was violently sick, on two, three or possibly seven separate occasions.

It's a strange feeling, to feel lonely and at the same time scared that somebody might talk to you. Gradually, after about ten hours or so, the loneliness started to win out. I became desperate to see someone, and my situation began to seem so insupportable that I considered, for the first time, going in and giving myself up to the police. Perhaps it would be best, after all, to make a clean breast of everything. Who knows, they might even have tracked down the real murderer by now, and I wouldn't be under any suspicion. They'd be pleased to see me, I'd be a valuable witness, and instead of finding myself on the threshold of a never-ending nightmare I'd be able to see the whole business wrapped up and disposed of, never to trouble me again. Oh God, if that could only be true.

I didn't have the courage to do it myself, of course. If I was going to give myself up I needed someone to help me, someone to take me along to the police station and be ready to back up my story. I only had one friend in London who could be relied upon to do that, and it was a lot to ask. An awful lot. But there was no choice, really. Not when you thought about it.

It took me another couple of hours to walk to Tony's house, which was in Shadwell. I kept close to the river as much as possible, and then headed up north when I reckoned I'd come far enough. It must have been getting on for ten-thirty by the time I got there. He and Judith had a new, fairly modern little place on a housing estate. I stood in the porch for ages, worried about the impression I would make as soon as they saw me, unable to imagine any coherent way of telling my story. I considered running away again. I hesitated, and wavered, and thought, and sweated, and shook. Finally I rang the bell.

Judith came to the door almost immediately. She was wearing her coat over what seemed (from the parts I could see) to be her smartest clothes, and her hair looked immaculate. Far from being surprised to see me, she gave every appearance of being relieved.

'William, there you are!' she said. 'We were starting to go frantic. We've been leaving messages on your machine all morning.' Before I had time to say anything she had turned around and was shouting up the stairs, 'It's all right, Tony, he's here!'

Tony came running downstairs. He was wearing a light grey suit with a narrow tie.

'Judith was convinced you'd forgotten,' he explained. 'We were a bit worried when we couldn't get you on the phone all night, you see. We thought you might have gone away for the weekend.'

'No, I was . . . round at Madeline's house last night,' I improvised, not entirely untruthfully. I didn't have a clue what was going on.

'Come into the kitchen,' said Judith, 'and I'll show you what's what.'

As I followed her into the kitchen, the explanation suddenly hit me. It was Sunday morning, and I was supposed to be looking after Ben for the day while they went up to Cambridge for their luncheon party: that promise I had made more than two weeks ago. As was only to be expected, I had forgotten all about it.

'There's some salad in the fridge,' Judith was saying, 'and some quiche. You and Ben are to help yourselves but don't give him any cucumber because he won't touch the stuff. Don't ask me why. He's at that sort of age. He'll show you how to work the video and he'll probably want you to play with him on his computer games. There's plenty of tea, and plenty of milk. He likes his milk with this strawberry stuff in it. It's very easy, you just have to stir it in.'

What could I do? I had been on the point of giving them a complete explanation – of narrating a more fantastic chain of events than I could ever have invented, in the hope that they would believe me and find some way of helping me out. But I couldn't do that now. Once again, circumstances were sweeping me away, carrying me beyond the realm where decisions could be made and free will exercised.

'He's in the sitting-room at the moment,' said Judith. 'He won't come out to see visitors. Don't ask me why. It's a phase he's going through. You'll find him ever so easy once you get talking to him. If he tries to throw things at you just give him a good smack. It usually works.'

Tony came into the kitchen, jingling the car keys.

'Come on, love, we're going to be late.'

Judith fetched her gloves and I followed them both to the front door.

'Feel free to use the piano,' said Tony. 'I don't think we'll be back any later than four.'

'Help yourself to biscuits,' said Judith.

'Play some records if you want,' said Tony.

'There's beer in the cupboard,' said Judith.

'Have a nice time,' I said. And then they were gone.

From the sitting-room I could hear a medley of little electronic pops and whistles and bubbling noises, which seemed to suggest that Benjamin was happily occupied with a video game. I put my head round the door just to make sure.

'Hi,' I said.

'Hello.'

I think Benjamin must have been about eight at this stage. He was a cute little child, with a healthy face and a cheerful disposition, and he already showed signs of his parents' intelligence. He never took his eyes off the television screen, but I didn't feel that he was being rude.

'I'm just going to go and play the piano.'

'Fine.'

Tony had a really lovely upright piano which he had bought cheap at a sale from the Royal College of Music or somewhere. I had only ever played it a couple of times and it had made even my worst improvisations sound reasonable. To be able to spend a whole day with this piano was an absolute treat, in other words, but as soon as I sat down at it and opened the lid, a curious thing happened: I found that I couldn't play. Even when I put my hands on the keys, chose a chord and took a deep breath, I couldn't bring myself to sound the notes. I must have done this nearly a dozen times. I thought of standards, I thought of originals, I thought of classical pieces – but I couldn't actually get any of them started. It was all too much. The murder, the flight from the police, that awful night in the cold, the realization that I was never going to see Madeline again – these things had been weighing down on me for too long, and all at once I caved in. I put my head in my hands and slumped forward on to the piano, and although I wasn't really crying, my body shook with sobs.

I don't think this lasted very long. The spasm soon passed, but I continued to lie across the keyboard, feeling oddly comfortable. I got up when I realized that Ben had come into the room and was staring at me. I don't know how long he had been there.

'I want to go for a walk,' he said, solemnly.

*

Once Ben was suitably wrapped up in his little duffle coat and woollen hat and gloves, we stepped outside and I locked up the house.

'Where do you want to go?' I asked.

'Let's go down to the basin.'

It wasn't a very good morning for a walk, in my opinion. It was far too cold, for one thing, and last night's mist hadn't entirely cleared yet. Of course, I also had my own reasons for not wanting to venture out, but I didn't see that much harm could come from a quick excursion if it was going to keep Ben happy. It might even help to calm me down, since playing the piano (my usual form of therapy) seemed to be out of the question at the moment. The bleakness of those East London streets, the strange misty chill which lay over the whole area, harmonized pleasingly with my mood. I felt that I could smell mystery on every corner, and I enjoyed hearing the occasional, random sounds of a quiet Sunday morning – cars starting, children shouting – and seeing the fog roll back, way in the distance, over the grey and restless Thames.

'Wow,' said Benjamin. 'What a *massive* piece of dog poo.'

I pulled him away from the offending object, which he had been inspecting with keen interest, and continued to hold his hand as we walked on. Before long, we found that we had come to a church: the vast, intimidating bulk of St George In The East.

'Is it true,' said Benjamin, as we walked past it, 'that criminals and people can go inside a church, and the police can't come and catch them?'

I stopped walking. I didn't know whether this was still true or not, although I remembered once being told the same thing, many years ago. Sanctuary. It seemed a straw worth clutching at.

'Let's go inside,' I said.

Benjamin, still holding my hand, seemed happy enough to follow me. As we got near to the doors I could hear the sound of ragged hymn-singing, but the thought that a service was in progress didn't deter me for more than a few seconds.

'Dad'll be so cross if he knows that you took me to church,' said Benjamin gleefully.

'Why?'

'He says that the church is a bourgeois conspiracy designed to preserve the existing social order.'

'Does he?' I said, rather taken aback. 'He should really leave you to work these things out for yourself, you know. Come on, anyway.'

We seemed to have arrived in the middle of a sung communion: the church was about half full (mainly with old people) and they were singing 'Immortal, Invisible', with the choir adding eccentric harmonies apparently designed to confuse the rest of the congregation. Ben and I settled down in a pew near the back and joined the hymn just in time for the last line. The service still had about twenty minutes to run but I don't think either of us paid very much attention to it. What I had said to Madeline all those months ago was true: I had been through a brief church-going phase when I was much younger (at the age when most of my friends were having adolescent love affairs – I don't know why I should have been different), but I wasn't religious by nature and my faith, such as it was, had faded away quickly and painlessly. The only thing I liked about religion now was the music it had inspired. So I didn't go up to take communion with the rest of the congregation, and most of the time my thoughts were far removed from the words of the priest: when they weren't spiralling around the events of the last twenty-four hours in a kind of daze, they were focused – oddly enough – on Benjamin.

He seemed to be poised between two different states, being both bored by the service and excited by the novelty of his unusual surroundings. Some of the time he squirmed in his seat and swung his legs restlessly over the edge of the pew; but sometimes he was content to settle against my side and stare up at the ceiling, or look around at the faces of the other worshippers, which presented a range of expressions from near-ecstasy to vacant inattention. The feeling of having a young child, trusting and dependent, resting at my side during a church service was (I need hardly say) the very last thing I had anticipated that morning. It was a long while, I realized, since I had spent any time at all in the company of children. I had shut myself off from even thinking about them. Had I ever fantasized, without admitting it to myself, about having children with Madeline? I tried to be honest, scratched around in the recesses of my most secret memories, but couldn't see that I had. No, the only person I had ever discussed it with – and I could remember the conversation now: shy, serious, playful – was Stacey.

Benjamin and I stayed put while the congregation was leaving. After a few minutes, we had the church to ourselves.

'Aren't we going to go now?' he asked.

'No. Let's stay a little longer.'

He got up and went on a brief tour of exploration. Even when he was out of sight, I could hear the echo of his footsteps as he ran backwards and forwards. It was one of those sounds – like the ringing of Mrs Gordon's doorbell – which drew attention to the surrounding silence. I made no attempt to follow him but continued to sit there thinking about Stacey.

Benjamin broke in upon my thoughts by tugging at my sleeve and saying, 'William. William.'

I looked up.

'What?'

He seemed on the verge of asking a question, but after a short pause he ran off giggling instead. Eventually he came and sat beside me again. I put my arm around him and when the weight of his body started to feel heavy I assumed he had fallen asleep. But then he said it again.

'William.'

'What?'

'Why were you crying in the back room?'

I glanced down at him, although for some reason I wasn't surprised by the question. His eyes were wide and enquiring.

'Well – without wishing to sound patronizing, I don't think you'd understand.'

'Men don't usually cry,' he said; but he said it to himself, as though, having decided that he wasn't going to get a truthful answer out of me, he was pursuing his own train of thought. 'Dad never cries. At least, only once, and that was Mum's fault.'

'Oh?' I said, mildly curious. 'Why was that?'

'She had a fling.' Benjamin was very matter of fact about this, and went on, 'She told Dad about it, and they had an argument, and he cried.'

I would never, never have believed that anything could make Tony cry. I tried to picture him in tears, weeping on Judith's shoulder, with Benjamin standing by the door, grave, unseen and watchful. It was the first time I had ever tried to picture Tony in a domestic setting; away from the piano.

'Was it something like that?' Benjamin asked.

'Well . . . yes,' I said, exasperated to find how good he was at drawing out confidences. 'I've been having a bit of trouble with a woman, if you must know.'

Benjamin paused, his mind busily running through the possibilities.

'Is it Auntie Tina?'

I shook my head.

'You don't know her. Her name's Madeline.'

As concisely as I could, I gave Benjamin a resumé of our affair, culminating in the scene at the party last night. Then we both fell silent. I thought, Well, at least that's shut him up.

'Is she tall?' he asked.

'What?'

'How tall is she?'

'I don't know . . . slightly above average, I suppose.'

'And what about Piers?'

'I suppose you'd call him tall. Six-one, six-two – something like that.' Suddenly I lost patience. 'Look, if you're suggesting that . . .'

Benjamin said nothing.

'Well, I suppose it's a thought . . .'

He got up.

'I'm cold. Let's go home and have dinner.'

He took me by the hand and we left the church, threading our way through the still backwaters of Shadwell, each absorbed in our thoughts. Benjamin was humming a tune to himself – it was 'I'm Beginning to See the Light', now I come to think of it, in his father's favourite E flat – and I was wondering, ridiculous though it seemed, and however hard I tried to fight against it, whether there might have been an absurd grain of truth in his theory. If it *was* the truth, it was a bitter one; but in a way, I felt comforted. Any explanation was better than none, after all.

I didn't attempt to play the piano again that day. When we got back to Tony's house we had some lunch and then watched television and played video games. I let Benjamin decide everything, except that I insisted on watching the local news bulletin. There was no mention of the murder. Perhaps time was not running out quite as fast as I'd thought.

Tony and Judith returned at about half past four. They seemed to have had a good time, and they could tell that Benjamin had enjoyed his afternoon with me, so they were profuse with their thanks. So much so, in fact, that Judith offered me a lift back to the flat.

'It's no trouble,' she said. 'Anyway, it's ages since I saw Tina properly.'

They must have been confused by my hesitation, but I think you can see why the prospect alarmed me. In my mind I had already put together a probable sequence of events which would have enabled the police to trace my address almost immediately. Chester and the band would have arrived at the recording studio; they would have waited for Paisley and me to turn up, with mounting impatience; finally Chester would have gone back to the house, swearing under his breath, only to find the place swarming with policemen. He would have been taken down to the station for questioning, and inevitably he would have told them that I was the last person to have seen Paisley alive. He would have given them my name, and told them where I lived. Without a shadow of a doubt, the police would be waiting for me at the flat.

But then, hadn't I decided to give myself up anyway? Wasn't that why I had come round to Tony's house in the first place? I'd felt that I needed his help to go through with it at the time, but now, after a few hours' rest, and after talking to Benjamin, I was stronger, clearer in the head, and I knew that I could do it alone. It would be a shock for Judith, admittedly; but at least her sister would be there (Tina would be worried already, with policemen coming round and asking where I was) and they could be of some comfort to each other until the whole business was cleared up.

And so I accepted her offer, and together we drove back to the Herbert Estate: Judith doing her best to make conversation, and me just gripping the sides of my seat tighter and tighter, my nervousness increasing steadily until by the time we were within a mile of our destination, I couldn't stop shaking. I nearly shouted out loud when we turned into the estate and the first thing I saw was a police officer standing on the balcony outside our flat. There were two police cars parked by our staircase as well. Even though I had been expecting it, it was a terrifying sight.

'Oh God,' said Judith. 'What's going on?'

'Stay here,' I said, once she'd parked the car. 'I'll go and see what the matter is.'

'No, I'm coming with you.'

We climbed the staircase and were stopped outside my door by a constable.

'Do you live at this flat?' he asked.

I nodded, told him my name, and said: 'Look, I know what you're thinking, but really I had nothing to do with it. I'm absolutely appalled by what happened and I can explain every – '

'It's all right,' he said reassuringly. 'You're not under any suspicion.'

'I'm not?'

I couldn't possibly describe the relief that flooded through me when I heard these words. It was so overwhelming that I barely listened to him as he continued: 'We just need you to answer a few questions, that's all. It's a messy business, this kind of thing, but it happens all the time, and the young lady's not in any danger any more – '

'Young *lady*?'

He stared at me.

'That's right. Young lady. You do know what I'm talking about, don't you?'

He took me inside, where there were two more police officers going through the contents of Tina's room. Apparently she had telephoned the ambulance service earlier that afternoon, to tell them that she had taken an overdose.

Judith took it very well, considering.

'We get dozens of these things,' said the constable. 'Literally dozens every week.' He was making a cup of tea for Judith, who sat, too shocked to move, at the kitchen table. 'It's a simple cry for help, really. Pure attention-seeking.' He gently handed her the mug, and said: 'Excuse me a moment, will you? Nature calls.'

Left alone, Judith and I found it hard to speak.

'I can't believe this,' I said. 'I can't believe it.'

I carried on saying useless things like that for some time, until she interrupted me. To my surprise, she sounded not grief-stricken but angry.

'How the hell could you let this happen, William? You're living with the woman, for Christ's sake.'

'Living with her? I never even *see* her.'

'Well weren't there any signs at all? Have you no idea what's going on?'

I was about to make another petulant denial; but I realized, of course, that Judith was right.

'There was this man . . .' I started.

Another policeman came into the kitchen.

'Could I have a word with you, please?'

We went into the sitting-room and he asked me a string of questions. I told him everything I knew about Pedro, all the fragments of information I had picked up about him, and I explained how Tina had been taking more and more days off work, and how she had looked last Sunday night, the last time I saw her.

A thought occurred to me.

'She didn't leave a note, did she?'

'As a matter of fact she did.'

He handed me a sheet of ruled A4: a fresh sheet, with only one message on it. It said:

Dear W, Please remember to lock the front door AND
BOLT IT when you come in tonight. I bought a nice
big loaf today so please help yourself. I don't think that
white stuff you eat is at all good for you. Can you write
me a cheque for the gas as I want to go and pay it on
Monday? Love, T.

I gave it back.

'There's one other thing,' he said. 'There was this

message on your answering machine. I don't suppose it has anything to do with what happened?'

He pressed the 'Play' button and there were the usual bleeps, followed by a woman's voice.

'Listen, William,' it said. 'About last night. I can explain everything.' A pause. 'I can explain everything, and get you out of trouble.' A longer pause. 'Come and see me at once.'

It clicked off.

'Well?'

'No,' I said, choosing my words carefully. 'That's a personal thing between me and . . . another woman.'

'Fine.'

He told me the name of the hospital and the number of the ward where Tina was being kept, and said that we could visit her immediately if we wanted. I must have thanked him, I suppose, but by this stage, as I showed him and his colleagues out of the flat, I didn't really know what I was saying. I was too busy wondering about that message. What did it mean?

And apart from anything else, how had Karla managed to find out my telephone number?

Coda

Gasping – but somehow still alive
this is the fierce last stand of all I am

MORRISSEY,
Well I Wonder

'I'm going out,' I said to Judith.

'You mean you're not coming with me to see Tina?'

It would have been pointless trying to explain. If it meant that her opinion of me plummeted even further, it was a problem I'd have to resolve at some other time. I simply left her the keys to the flat and told her to send Tina my love. As she watched me leave, her eyes burned with indignation.

It was quite dark by now. I ran all the way to London Bridge station, caught a tube to the Angel, and was standing outside the video shop in less than half an hour. Next to this shop, there was an unnumbered door, painted blue. It seemed likely that this would lead to the flats on the first and second floors. There was a man leaning against the door, a short, swarthy-looking man who wore steel-rimmed spectacles and was chewing gum. His hair was dark, tousled and curly. As I approached, he straightened himself, blocked the doorway and stared at me until I felt compelled to say: 'I've come to see Karla.'

I thought he was never going to answer.

'Name?' he said at last.

'William.'

He turned and rang one of the bells. The flats were equipped with an entrocom system, and before long the speaker crackled and Karla's voice said, 'Yes?'

'William,' said the man.

'All right.'

The door was opened for me, and I climbed four flights of narrow, tatty stairs. They led to a small landing where there were three doors, one of which was ajar. From behind this door, Karla's voice said: 'Come in, William.'

I pushed the door open. It was a gloomy bedsitting-room, practically unfurnished. There was no carpet and there were no decorations on the walls. An armchair took up one corner of the room, next to a washbasin and a mirror. There was a chest of drawers, an iron bed and a little three-legged table. Karla was sitting on the bed.

'I just got your message,' I said, when it became clear that she wasn't going to speak to me.

'Good.'

Her gaze was searching, as if she was trying to deduce some inner secret from my outward behaviour.

'I didn't realize you had my phone number,' I faltered, after an even longer pause.

'No.'

She seemed different, very different, from the woman who worked behind the bar at The White Goat. She was morose and aggressive but I got the impression that there was furious activity going on inside her head at that moment. I began to wonder, in fact, whether she wasn't just as confused as I was.

'Are you going to explain?' I asked.

'Perhaps you should explain.'

'Me?'

'Yes, William. You.'

I shrugged nervously.

'I don't know what you mean.'

'Now look, you're in a hell of a lot of trouble. The police are looking everywhere for you, in case you didn't know. I told you that I can help you, but I need to know what you're up to first.'

'I'm not up to anything,' I protested. 'I'm a musician, that's all.'

'Are you on his side?'

'Whose side? What are you talking about?'

Furious, she got up and advanced towards me. I hadn't realized how tall she was.

'Look – I know you've been following me. You admitted as much yourself that night in the pub. And the same night you tried to scare me by having that record lying on the table. You've been working with him, too. I know you have. And then you miraculously turn up in the house, just in time to see this guy – Paisley – get killed. So what's going on?'

'I don't know,' I said: it was almost a whimper. 'I don't know.'

Karla glared at me, then went to the chest of drawers and brought out an envelope from the bottom drawer. She took out a large black and white photograph and held it up in front of my face.

'You recognize *this*, don't you?'

'Yes,' I said. It was the photograph from the record sleeve, showing the figure of a woman looking out over a stretch of river, flanked by the two dwarves.

'And what about this?'

She showed me a second photograph, and I stared at it in amazement. It was the same scene. But the woman had turned around, and was now clearly recognizable – in spite of her cropped, bleached hair – as a younger version of Karla. And the two little figures, who had taken off their hoods, were not dwarves at all. They were two children: small girls, identical in size and appearance, smiling warmly at the camera.

'This is you?'

She nodded.

'And that was . . . *you* – singing on the record?' I asked, recalling the voice which had screamed its way through those two hideous songs.

'Yes.'

Karla walked to the mirror and took off her wig of thick, auburn hair. She turned to face me. Her hair was even shorter, now, than in the photograph: a close crew-cut on top, shaved at the sides and back.

'There,' she said, coming closer. 'Now do I look more like a killer?'

I backed away.

'But – you didn't kill Paisley?'

'That was a mistake. Those fucking idiots: I should had done the whole thing myself. I *will* do it myself. He's not going to get away again. Christ, I've waited long enough . . .'

She sat down on the bed, and fell silent.

'Who's not going to get away?' I asked. 'And who are these children?' I was so bewildered by now, I couldn't get the questions out quickly enough. 'Who did you send to get Paisley? Was it those brothers from Glasgow – the same people you named the band after?'

Karla didn't answer: not for a long time. And when she did finally start to explain, her speech was tired and slow.

'There was never any "band" called The Dwarves of Death,' she said. 'It was just me and my husband. I did the singing and he played the instruments: it was all put together in the studio. We were broke – as usual – and we thought we'd cash in on the whole punk thing and try to make a bit of extra money. We were living in Glasgow, then, and you wouldn't believe how poor we were. We did the recordings in the evenings. I was going out to work every day, doing cleaning jobs. He didn't have a job, he stayed at home looking after the kids.' She pointed to them in turn. 'Claire, and Sandra. We had twins.'

The bed was covered by a single threadbare quilt. From beneath this, she produced a sawn-off, double-barrelled shotgun, and a box of cartridges. She started to load the gun as she talked.

'And then, one day, Sandra disappeared. She ran away from home. And that was when Claire came to me, and told me what their . . . father . . . had been doing to them, while I was out all day.' She gave the word 'father' a bitter inflexion, as if it was a bad taste that had to be spat out. 'I don't suppose you want me to go into the details, do you? A doctor examined her, anyway, and confirmed her story. But I never saw Sandra again. The police found a body a few weeks later. It might have been hers, I couldn't tell. As for Claire . . .' She got up and went to the window, leaving the gun, now fully loaded, lying on the bed, ' . . . she grew up into quite a kid. She's in this "home" now. This centre. I don't go and see her. She won't talk to me.'

As Karla's story unfolded, her voice was getting harder and faster.

'Needless to say, when all this came to light, he lost no time in clearing out. He vanished into thin air that night and didn't leave a trace. I could only think of one way of getting a message to him, and that was why I did that song, "Insomnia". We'd just recorded a new single, you see, but we hadn't done the B-side yet. So one night I just went into the studio and let all the rage and hatred come out. I knew he'd have to buy the record when he saw it, and I wanted to make sure he knew that I was going to track him down. I put that picture on the sleeve, too. We used to dress the girls up in these little hoods and use them in publicity shots. People started to think they were actually members of the band. I wanted that picture to haunt him. I wanted him to know what it meant: that I was going to find him one day. Find him and kill him.'

From the little table, she picked up a small, plastic, rectangular object: it was a cassette.

'It took me years to track him down. He'd been in Europe most of the time. I followed a false lead and spent months in Canada and America. Then when I'd found him, it took me another year to raise the money to have him killed the way I wanted him killed. It cost me twenty thousand pounds.'

Dreading the answer (because I knew it already), I asked: 'And where did you find him?'

'He was running a studio complex in South London.'

She threw me the tape. It was a copy of our demo containing 'Madeline (Stranger in a Foreign Land)'.

'Vincent,' I said.

'That seems to be what he calls himself these days. He was Duncan when I married him.'

I looked at the tape and frowned.

'How did you get this?'

'It was in Paisley's pocket. Luckily they got blood all over his jacket and had to bring it back here: otherwise the police would really have had no trouble finding you. You even took the precaution of giving your phone number.'

I said nothing, shocked into silence by the thought of all the repercussions, all the ripples set in motion by the recording of this simple song only a week ago.

'I see that he produced it for you,' said Karla. 'There's a bit too much reverb on the vocals for my liking. He always made the same mistake.'

'I still don't understand why the police haven't caught up with me,' I said. 'Surely they've spoken to Chester by now? Hasn't he told them where I live?'

Karla laughed.

'Chester? He's more slippery than you give him credit for. I should imagine that when he got back last night and saw all those policemen, he made a run for it. It'll be a while before anyone hears from him again.'

'Him and Vincent,' I said, ' – what's the connection, then?'

'Business, basically.' Karla produced a pair of heavy black boots from under the bed and started to put them on. 'A man like Duncan – Vincent – doesn't make his living from running a rehearsal studio. Most of his money comes from heroin. Chester does odd jobs for him in that line now and again, but he's small fry by comparison. His other big field is property. He's got his hands on a lot of houses in the Islington area, mainly through crooked contracts. That's why Paisley and friends were living in one of them.'

'How did you find all this out?'

'It wasn't easy,' she said, as she finished tying her laces. 'I knew a lot of this stuff was based at The White Goat, although Duncan himself was too clever to be seen there. So I had to sweet-talk the manager into giving me a job, and then one of the guys behind the bar got me this flat.'

Karla filled in the other gaps for me as she got ready to go out. She'd tracked down the two little brothers from Glasgow, who'd been released from prison a couple of years earlier, and offered them five thousand pounds to carry out the killing. They agreed to do it for twenty. She told them what to wear, and even what position they were to take up just before they made their attack. Everything was calculated to recall the promise she had made on that record, and to fill Vincent with as much terror as possible in the few moments before he died. (I remembered, now, the strange way he had reacted to those two children, wearing matching anoraks, who had come into the studio one morning and scared the life out of him.) She knew that The Unfortunates would be out of the house on Saturday night, and she entrusted one of the brothers with the job of contacting Vincent by phone to make sure he would be there. It was only Paisley's intervention which had made the scheme backfire.

'Were you there last night?' I asked. 'Was it you driving the car?'

'No,' she said. 'That was the guy you saw downstairs. He's just someone I hired. He was recommended to me:

does a lot of this sort of work, apparently. He's going to drive us to the studio now.'

I felt a tremor of apprehension.

'What do you mean, drive *us*?'

'You don't think I called you over here just to put your mind at rest, do you?' said Karla, bundling the shotgun and more cartridges into a black holdall. 'You're going to help me.'

'Me? How?'

'I'm going to go into that studio and kill him. Right now, this evening. But I need someone who knows his way around, and you've been there before. I've heard the place is like a labyrinth. He mustn't get away.'

'Now look – ' I started backing towards the door. 'I'm sorry about what happened to you, you've been through some . . . terrible things. But I have to say I think you're going about this in completely the wrong way.'

Karla was looking at me in disbelief.

'However,' I continued, 'in the light of what you've told me, I'll make a deal with you: let me go and I promise I won't tell the police anything about it.'

She reached into her holdall and took out the shotgun.

'Shut the fuck up,' she said. 'You're coming with me or I blow your brains out.'

I took a deep breath and nodded.

'Fine.'

I'd never had anyone aim a gun at me before: as an aid to decision-making, I'd say it can't be bettered. I stood transfixed by the sight of Karla pointing this thing at my chest. When she saw how frightened I was, she started to chuckle and push me downstairs.

'What are you laughing at?' I said.

She chuckled even more.

'You and your bloody folk songs.' She prodded me in the back with the rifle. 'Sorry, pal. I'm no Mary O'Hara.'

She put the gun away in her bag before we got outside, and then grabbed me by the arm and propelled me out into the street. It was a black, cold night, and there was nobody around to see us. Our driver was waiting by the doorway, and the three of us walked, without speaking, down to his car which was parked on the Essex Road. Karla and I sat on the back seat. She took the shotgun out of her bag and laid it on her lap, and from the pocket of her jeans she took out a piece of paper which had the address of Thorn Bird Studios written on it.

'This is where we're going,' she said to the driver. 'Now step on it.'

He took the piece of paper and turned to her, looking puzzled.

'Step on it?'

'Not the paper, stupid. I mean hurry. *Rápido!*'

'Ah.'

He started the car and drove off at a furious pace. I thought for a moment about what Karla had just said. A new, astonishing suspicion was creeping over me.

'What did you say to him?' I asked.

'*Rápido*. It's Spanish for "quick".'

Her eyes were bright with anticipation, now, and she

was tapping both her feet excitedly. It scared me to see how much she was looking forward to the task ahead of her: the fulfilment, I suppose, of a craving which had been burning inside her for years. She certainly didn't look as though she felt like answering any more questions; but I had to ask, in a whisper: 'Is he Spanish?'

'That's right. His name's Pedro.'

She continued to fix me with this mocking, teasing, irrepressible smile. At any other time, and in any other woman, it would have been captivating. I beckoned her closer and whispered in her ear: 'I *know* him.'

'You do?'

'He's been seeing my flatmate. He's an absolute bastard.'

'Really?' She pretended to look amazed. 'And I only hired him because he seemed such a nice sort of bloke.'

All the indignation I felt about what he'd done to Tina started to boil over, suddenly. Back at the flat, it had been held in check by a level of panic and mystification which wouldn't allow room for any other feelings. Now it welled up into a kind of hatred.

'He's been giving my flatmate hell,' I whispered. 'Doing terrible things to her. She even tried to kill herself.'

'Too bad,' said Karla flatly.

'If I could just have five minutes alone with him . . .'

She looked at me, smiling again.

'What would you do?'

This was a difficult question.

'I'd . . . give him a really good talking to.'

She permitted herself a quiet but emphatic laugh, and then turned her gaze on Pedro.

'Well, let's see if we can do better than that,' she said.

We drove along in silence for a few more minutes. Then Karla leant forward and tapped Pedro on the shoulder.

'Nearly there?' she asked.

'Nearly. I think so.'

'I suppose when we get there you'll want to be paid, eh, Pedro?'

'That's right. When we get there.'

'And how much was I going to pay you again? Five thousand, wasn't it?'

'That's right, five thousand pounds. Cash in the nail.'

She drew in her breath.

'Five thousand pounds – that's a lot of money, isn't it?'

He giggled stupidly.

'It is, *señora*. It's a lot of money.'

'What are you going to do with all that money?'

He giggled again.

'I don't know. Maybe I'll be going back to Spain.'

'Is there someone waiting for you out in Spain, eh, Pedro? Some little Spanish *señorita*?'

He grinned and fondled his stubbly chin.

'Maybe. Maybe there is someone, yes.'

'But I bet that hasn't stopped you from having a bit of fun while you were over here, eh, Pedro? We all like a bit of fun, don't we?'

'That's right, *señora*,' he said, laughing. 'We all like a bit of fun.'

I interrupted them. 'You turn left here. The studio's only about fifty yards up the next road.'

'OK. Stop the car here, Pedro. Stop the car.'

We were parked in the darkest and most deserted of back alleys. Pedro turned off all the lights.

'So are you going to get her a present before you leave, Pedro? A present for your little bit of fun?'

'I don't know. Maybe I will.'

He was grinning again, and his teeth, reflected in the driver's mirror, looked yellow and shiny in the darkness.

'Does she know what you do for a living, this girl, Pedro? I bet you didn't tell her what you really do.'

'That's right,' he said, between more of those stupid giggles.

'What did you tell her, then? What does she think you do?'

'She thinks I drive cars. You know, for passengers.'

'You're an old dog, aren't you, Pedro, eh?' said Karla, provoking fits of laughter. 'You're a bit of an old rascal, aren't you?'

'That's right. I am a bit, yes.'

'Now – I've got this little problem, Pedro, which is that I can't give you all the money right now. I'm going to have to give you something else, to be going on with.'

'Something else?'

He turned, and she leant very close to his face.

'Something else. Do you know what I mean?'

His long, slow smile spread itself again.

'I think I do. I think maybe I do.'

'You like British girls, don't you, Pedro?'

'Oh yes. I like them very much.'

'This other British girl – I bet she'd do anything you asked her to, wouldn't she?'

More giggles. 'Well . . . she'd do a lot of things. And sometimes, you know, what's wrong with a little . . .'

'Gentle persuasion?'

'That's right.'

'A bit of pressure?'

'Yes.'

Karla raised the shotgun to the level of his head.

'Pedro,' she said. 'You're a waste of space.'

The noise of the shot was deafening, and – well, I've never seen anything like what happened then. His head exploded. Literally. It went everywhere. Bits of Pedro were splattered all over the windscreen, the dashboard, the seat covers, the roof. Blood shot in all directions and I got drenched in the stuff. In was in my hair, warm and sticky, and it was on my face and on my coat and on my hands. I was covered in Pedro. He was all over me. I must have been screaming or crying or some thing because suddenly Karla hit me in the face and shouted: 'Shut up! Shut the fuck up! Now get out of the car!'

She pushed me out of the car and I fell into the street. Then she dragged me up off the floor and started pulling me along with her. I looked back at the car. The driver's door was open – he must have grabbed the handle just as he realized what she was going to do to him – and what was left of Pedro was lying, half in and half out, slumped against the kerb. When Karla saw that I was looking back she struck me in the face again and pushed me on.

We reached the main door of Thorn Bird Studios, which she kicked open. I went in ahead of her. It seemed light and warm inside, almost homely. Vincent was sitting behind his desk drinking a cup of tea and reading a Sunday magazine. Seeing me, covered in blood, shaking, barely able to stand, he dropped the magazine and got to his feet. He was about to say something when Karla appeared. They stared at each other for perhaps three or four seconds: it was the first time he had seen her in ten years. Then she said, 'This is for Sandra. And this is for Claire,' and fired twice.

Both shots missed.

She lunged at him, then; but with a show of unexpected strength he lifted up the desk and shoved it at her. Thrown off balance, she fell to the ground.

'Follow him, you bastard, follow him.'

Vincent had made a dash for it down an unlit corridor. I found the time-switch and slammed it on just in time to see him disappear round a corner. Karla pushed past me, nearly knocking me over, and without stopping to ask myself why, I followed her.

The pursuit can't have lasted more than a couple of minutes. Every few seconds the lights would go off and the corridors would be thrown into darkness, and I'd have to grope frantically for the nearest switch: I knew that Vincent could find his way just as easily in the dark. He took us up and down all those countless little staircases until we were dizzy and hopelessly disorientated. Finally, it seemed as though we had lost him altogether. We stood there, panting in the darkness, straining to hear his footsteps above the muffled noise of bands practising in the adjacent rehearsal rooms.

'Shit,' said Karla. 'SHIT!'

Then I found a light switch and turned it on: and there was Vincent, at the far end of the corridor, struggling to unlock the door of Studio B. Before we could get there he had slipped inside and closed the door behind him.

The lights went out again. I put a restraining hand on Karla's arm and took a few breaths.

'We've got him,' I said. 'He can't lock the studio door from inside.'

'Are you sure?'

'Yes.'

'What's in there?'

'I don't know.'

She shook free of my hand and stepped back.

'Then we'll soon find out.'

But now I did an amazing thing. I said, 'Hold on', and blocked her way. Some maniacal form of bravado seemed to have possessed me, and I heard myself saying, 'I'll go in first.' When this suggestion met with incredulous silence, I added: 'It might be dangerous.'

In one swift, decisive movement, I pulled open the door of Studio B, and charged.

If I had stopped to look down, just for a second, I

would have seen that there was a narrow iron ladder fixed to the wall. It led to a little landing-stage from which, sometimes, the shouts of sailors would rise up into the night air as they loaded and unloaded their boats. But I didn't stop. I caught a sudden glimpse of clouds skimming over the face of a lambent moon, and plunged headlong into the ink-black ice-cold waters of the Thames.

Fade

and everybody's got to live their life
and God knows I've got to live mine

God knows I've got to live mine

MORRISSEY,
William, It Was Really Nothing

If you leave the main road as it curves around The Fox House pub, and head downhill, through the woods, you soon come to a wide, fast-moving stream. It can be crossed at various points. There are stepping stones, for the agile, and there are two wooden footbridges; pausing here, you can watch the bubbling water through gaps between the planks. As you walk further down, the terrain becomes wilder. Huge rocks and felled trees lie at the borders of the stream, and just before the path begins to shelve steeply into dense woodland you can turn, and above you is a magnificent ridge; your eye lingers on this bare, sweeping landscape, fixing on the point where the earth gives way to sky and the palest of blues lights up the horizon. There are other walkers about, but it is quiet: you might almost say silent.

'I love it here,' said Stacey.

'It's beautiful,' I agreed.

'Beats London, doesn't it?' said Derek.

I squatted down by the edge of the stream, running my fingers through the water. Dew was still thick on the ground and the breeze was heady with the scent of spring.

'Anything beats London.'

Coming home had been the easiest thing in the world, after all. The first day I felt able to go out again – about a week or two after my return – I had climbed one of Sheffield's highest hills, watched the whole city as its lights began to spread with the onset of dusk, and it had seemed incredible that I could have lived without the place for so long. It seemed warm and gentle and clean. And I had come to cherish the nearness of the countryside, to spend days retracing all my old walks, finding a new companionship in the dales whose friendship I had once been foolish enough to snub. More often than not, I would take these walks alone; but today I had asked Stacey and Derek to come with me. It was Sunday morning, the first really good Sunday of spring.

I heard her whisper: 'You don't have to keep reminding him.'

'You don't seem to realize,' I said, 'that I'm getting over it.'

'He's a tough kid, our William,' said Derek. He started to climb a tree but got stuck half-way up.

'Are you going to go down and see Tina soon?' Stacey asked, taking advantage of his absence.

'I don't even have her new address.'

All I knew was that she had moved into a flat somewhere near Wimbledon, sharing with two other women. When Judith had given me this and no other information, I took it to be her way of hinting that I should keep my distance for a while.

'Don't feel guilty, William.'

I turned, and she was smiling at me. We stood like that for a while, on opposite sides of the path. Then there was a violent rustle of leaves and Derek jumped down from the tree, landing between us with a strangled cry. Stacey screamed and started laughing.

'You scared me.'

'Do you still have nightmares, William?' Derek asked, as we walked on. He ignored her reproving glances.

'Now and then.'

'What would you do,' he said, 'if I told you that your worst nightmare was about to come true?'

'Derek! Shut up!'

I considered: 'Like what?'

'They never found them, did they? Either of them.'

'No.'

'So Vincent could be . . . hiding behind that rock. And Karla could be waiting for us at the bottom of the hill.'

'In theory. What of it?'

He clutched my shoulder with a claw-like hand, and said in a hoarse theatrical whisper: 'Let me tell you; something worse, something infinitely worse is about to happen.'

I looked blank.

'Didn't you read about it in the paper?'

'What?'

'There's a new Andrew Lloyd Webber musical opening in London this month.'

I groaned happily and pushed him away.

'London's miles off. I can cope with that.'

Derek took Stacey in his arms. He lifted her into the air and, twirling around, they enjoyed a long and energetic kiss while I studied the lichen formations on a nearby boulder. I suppose in my heart I still hadn't quite come to terms with it.

'Derek, will you *stop* giving William a hard time,' she said, as he dropped her none too carefully on to the ground.

'Well, I haven't forgiven him for losing my bloody record yet.'

'I told you, I don't mind,' I said. For a moment the phrase reminded me of Madeline, but I hastily brushed the memory aside. 'Anyway, I'm beginning to look on the whole thing as a . . . learning experience.'

'You've grown up, I can tell you that,' said Derek. 'Not your body, unfortunately, but the rest of you has.'

I couldn't find anything to throw at him so I said: 'Do you really think so?'

'Definitely. I reckon another fifteen years and you'll be reaching puberty.'

Even then, all I did was smile. It's a funny thing, actually, but these days I can't seem to get enough of being teased.